Crashpad

James R. Preston

Crashpad by James R. Preston

Cover design by Heather Swaim

Rendrag Publishing 10/3/17
ISBN: 978-0-9911516-4-6 (sc)
ISBN: 978-0-9911516-5-3 (ebook)

Here's where Napoleon pulled his Bonaparte.

-- Men's Room Graffiti,
Long Beach State (ca. 1969)

The Girl at the Door

It was arterial spray from her roommate Becky that saved Mary Jane's life. There was so much blood he must have thought she was dead too. Mary Jane lay utterly still under the warm corpse of her friend. She could hear the shooter in the living room, tearing books off shelves, swearing, muttering, occasionally chuckling. He'd made her undress so he could search her clothes, he said, but she knew it was just because he could. She knew a lot about him. Then he'd shot them both. Just held the sawed-off on them with one hand, pinched out his joint with the other, popped the roach in his mouth, chewed briefly, swallowed, and pulled the trigger. Because the only light in the room came from a bubbling lava lamp, he thought he'd hit them both. That and the fact that he was stoned. Stoned and desperate and armed. Not a good combination. That thought kept repeating itself inside her head. Stoned and desperate and armed. Not a good combination. He'd pulled the trigger, and they'd both gone down, Becky on top, clutching at the bedspread as her knees buckled and they fell, pulling the brown cloth partially over them, covering their legs and hips as if they were sharing a bed in the crashpad and it was hot so one of them had kicked the covers partly off. Now she was on the floor, Becky was dead, and everything had gone wrong. Becky's wiglet had come unfastened in the fall, and strands of brown wig hair blew across her face and throat, a piece getting stuck in the thick river of blood that flowed from her neck and over her cheek. Becky would have hated that; she was always so careful about her appearance.

The noises of the search in the other room stopped. All she could hear was the Doors' "Light My Fire" on the stereo and a game show on the TV. In the crashpad, they were both on constantly, one as some kind of demented counterpoint to the other. Quickly she scooped more of Becky's blood and let it drip across her face and chest. Then she exhaled sharply, closed her eyes, and hoped.

On the day that all of the wonderful things happened to him, Walter Darlymple was thinking about lasers and Green Lantern. He slept till noon, when pounding on the door of his apartment woke him up.

It was a good thing he slept late, because that meant he didn't see the screaming headlines about the dead guy found yesterday on the college campus, stuffed into the metal-lined trench that led up to the modern sculpture called *Hardfact*.

He waited, thinking that Arlen or Marty had to be home and would answer. The pounding on the door had to be for one of them; his parents had visited a week ago, bringing half a ham, a casserole dish full of potatoes au gratin, and a letter from the University of California at Berkeley. His mother had opened the letter at home and told him the news while she was putting the ham and potatoes in their otherwise bare refrigerator. The admissions office said his credits were good and his test scores exceptional and he could transfer—but here his mother looked at his father on the couch, and his father said, "Why would you want to go so far away from home?"

Then she said, "Let the boy decide. You weren't much older when you went overseas."

The pounding on the apartment door went on, and Walt gave up. He got out of bed, carefully stepping around the stacks of plastic-wrapped comics that were lined up in precise rows across the shag carpet, and shuffled out into the living room, yawning. He was tugging an ochre Cal State Long Beach sweatshirt over his head, so it took him a minute before he pulled it all the way down, opened the door, and saw the naked blonde girl standing in front of him. A moment later, he realized that she wasn't *totally* naked; she had on white knee-high boots and a pair of white bikini underpants. Her arms were covering her breasts. A moment—a long moment—after that, he realized she was talking.

"Um, what? What did you say? Never mind, I don't care. Yes, certainly, come right in." He forgot to step aside, so she pushed past him into the apartment and shoved a hip into the door to slam it closed.

"He's got a shotgun, and he killed Becky, and he's come back, and now he wants to kill me."

"What? Who? I was asleep, and I have a slow-starting metabolism. Never mind. Who are you? Wait, do you live upstairs?"

He finally looked at her face: wide brown eyes, blond hair in a flip, bangs, full lips covered with hot pink lipstick.

"You jumped out of a cake and got locked out of the party?"

She grabbed his shoulders. "Gun! Gun! He's got a gun." Since, in order to grab his shoulders, she had to move her arms away from her breasts, it took a moment for Walter to understand what she was saying or, for that matter, that she was talking at all.

His name was Walter Dalrymple, and he was an eighteen-year-old sophomore at Cal State Long Beach. He had skipped two grades and would have skipped another had his mother not put her foot down, telling the guidance counselor and his father, "The boy needs to stay with his friends," and in later years, when he thought of such things, Walter thought that single statement defined his relationship with both his parents. She wanted to do the best for him; they both did—her grim and determined, him focusing on the boy in between supervising corporate audits. They wanted him to be happy and successful. The thing was, neither of them knew that he had no friends. Sitting in Lecture Hall 151 with a hundred strangers at Cal State Long Beach would be like sitting in class with kids he recognized from the halls at Morningside High, but who were strangers. *Exactly* like sitting in that dusty classroom.

"Initiation, right? What sorority?" There was a joke sorority name, somebody had said it in the cafeteria last week. It was really funny, but he couldn't remember it. He thought, correctly, that neither of his roommates would believe him when he told them about this. He wished he had one of those instant cameras so he could set it on the timer and take their picture.

Walter, raised a gentleman, pulled off his sweatshirt and handed it to his visitor. She nodded thanks and slipped it over her head. He started to speak, but she clapped her hand over his mouth. Her scent when she stood close was wonderful.

There was the sound of heavy feet outside. Then someone was pounding on the door, hard enough to rattle the cheap wood in its frame.

"Out! Come out of there! Come out now!"

"Are you sure you have the right apartment?" But something made him whisper. The door shook under pounding fists. He looked at her again and decided. Walter Dalrymple was many things, but slow was not one of them. It was either a gag or it wasn't. Playing along meant the blonde would stay in his apartment longer, maybe even until his roommates came back. It would be great if Arlen or Marty saw him with a girl in the apartment.

She didn't look scared, not exactly, but her eyes—wonderful, he loved her eyes—were darting around the small living room. The apartment was a two-bedroom, two-bath in a building located across Bellflower Boulevard from Cal State Long Beach, called Beachi Tiki, and naturally, it catered to college students. He pulled her hand off his mouth, grabbed her arm, and dragged her into his bedroom, carefully guiding her around the stacks of comics. His father had brought the last of his collection, and he had been sorting and bagging yesterday afternoon until his time in the lab came around. She looked at Batman and Robin struggling to the top of a mountain called K2 to retrieve a spool of microfilm, and he blushed. He opened the closet and pointed at his clothes hamper. She whispered, "No way. I won't fit." It was a big wicker hamper pushed up against the wall of the closet, but there was no room for even a small girl, and she wasn't.

"Step in. Slide your, uh, slide down, and as you do, extend your legs into the space on the other side of the wall. Quick!" She stepped in, bent her knees, and slid down. Gripping the sides of the hamper for support, she stuck out her feet and looked at him, wide-eyed, as they did not find the edge of the hamper or the wall of the closet but instead extended into a space between the walls. He went to his chest of drawers, grabbed what he could, and dumped shirts on top of her. Then he took a quick look around the room, debated hiding the comics, and went to the door.

The man on the other side was no taller than Walter, but he was twice as wide. The word that popped into Walter's mind was "Fireplug." His eyes were bloodshot, he had a three-day growth of beard, and he reeked of pot and sweat with a dash of beer. Black hair, parted on the left, hung down in his face.

"What? What's with all the yelling? I'm trying to sleep here."

"Where's the girl?"

"I don't know. Wait, did you bring one? My roommates will be back any minute." Walter thought that it was good to let this guy know other people were on their way.

Dark, piggy eyes focused on him. The eyes were so red they looked like there were no whites at all. "Where is she?"

"I thought you were bringing her."

Walter looked at the stranger's face, and all at once, like switching off the burning streak of coherent light that he was studying, it wasn't fun. It wasn't fun at all. He knew that the blonde hiding in his closet was not kidding, that this was not a prank, and that he was in serious danger.

You develop an instinct when you are the playground punching bag, when, at recess, you know to stay close to the teacher so that when you get pushed down, at least you don't get the ever-popular Indian rope burn as a little bonus, or get rolled onto your back, knees on your biceps, and rocked back and forth to grind muscles and tendons together. And those are the kids that are pretty much okay, the ones that will hurt you but not seriously and who will honestly think it was all just in fun. It's the other kind you learn to *really* watch out for, the fortunately rare ones who will send you to the nurse's office, the ones with blank faces and eyes that hate with or without reason, as if hate is all there is for them and that really pisses them off because they know other kids feel something else, something that must be good, and shit, if I can't have it, neither will anybody.

The fireplug at the door was one of those. Walter sensed that he had learned to mask it, to pretend to experience things like love and friendship, but that those things were as unknown to him as the far side of the moon. When you're the school punching bag, you learn to see things like that.

The stranger slammed a palm into Walt's shoulder, spinning him around, sending him reeling, before he kicked the door shut and quickly searched the apartment. He was back in a minute, saying, "Okay, did a girl try to hide here?"

"You mean you weren't kidding?"

"Blonde. Not wearing much."

"I think I would have noticed."

"Hopeless. You're fucking hopeless."

"Can I go back to sleep now?"

Fireplug stretched his mouth into a grin. "Sorry to have bothered you." He paused. "Wait. PS I love you."

"What?"

"Mean anything to you?"

"I don't know, what—"

The fireplug grabbed Walt and shook him. He was so strong it was as if Walt was a rag doll. His fingers dug into Walt's bare shoulders. His breath was foul. "Song! It's a Beatles song!" He let go and scratched absently at his cheek before crossing his arms. "Hopeless." Scratched his head. "Sorry to have bothered you. Do yourself a favor, kid, and don't tell nobody."

"Sure, no problem. If this girl comes by, what should I tell her? Would you like to leave a message?"

Fireplug just stared at him. He took one last look around, stepped into Walter's room, and kicked the largest stack of comics—it happened to be Walter's *Green Lantern* collection—sending them across the floor, accompanied by the sound of ripping paper. "Oh, gee, sorry about that."

He ran out, slamming the door behind him.

Walter fought back tears, for the *Green Lanterns* but more for the fact that the tears were there—for a stack of comic books—and most of all for the fact that she might see them. So he fought hard.

Walt turned and hurried into his room in time to see her as she sort of shimmied and squirmed to stand up and step out of the hamper. She said, "Clean shirts," and she held them out to him. "Not many dirty clothes."

"Friday is laundry night."

"Oh. Wow, thanks, man. You saved my life."

He clapped his hand over her mouth and then pulled free as if he'd been given an electric shock. Urgently he pointed at the hamper. She climbed in and pulled the lid closed just as the front door was thrown open and fireplug was back.

There was a long strand of blonde hair sticking out from under the lid of the hamper.

Walter snatched up the *Green Lanterns* and held them out. "Look what you did!" He was standing in front of the open closet door and the hamper. The shirts that had been in the hamper were now piled on his bed. Bad if fireplug noticed.

"Aw, gee." Fireplug slapped the comics out of Walter's hands and said, "If she comes here—never mind. No chance." He looked around, squinting, and then left again. Walter trotted to the door and listened, watching to see if the light from the peephole was eclipsed.

After a few minutes, she climbed out again.

"How did you know?"

"How did I know what?"

"That he'd come back?"

Walter shrugged. "Lucky guess. Who was that guy?"

"What's the deal with the trick hamper? You guys need to hide out a lot?"

"The kids who lived here before were dealers, nothing big, just pot and a few reds, but they had unpleasant visitors, so they cut a hole in the wall and the side of the hamper for emergencies. They got busted before they ever used it. So, you live upstairs? I haven't seen you before."

"No, not really. I crash there once in a while." She took a deep breath. "A girl has been shot."

"Shot?" Walter heard the word, and of course, his brain processed it, but there was no connection to his reality, the world of experiments, black and white speckled lab books, and it's Friday night so the laundromat won't be crowded.

"Upstairs, in the crashpad."

Oddly, Walter's brain picked that moment to tell him he'd forgotten his slippers. His feet were cold. But it was a good brain, and after a moment, it kicked into gear. "Is she..."

"Dead? Oh, yeah. Where's your phone?"

They both heard the door open again. The girl darted toward the closet, blonde hair flying as she danced around the comics. Walt went out to see his roommates, Arlen and Marty, plopping down on the couch. When they saw him, they jumped to attention and saluted. Walt grinned. He had known them both since high school, and since graduation, they had gone from a couple of guys who were distinguished by not stuffing him into trash cans and looking to him for homework help to the closest approximation to friends that he had. If they sometimes teased him and played pranks, that was okay. Arlen was short and pudgy. He desperately wanted to be a surfer and was dressed, as usual, in a striped Hang Ten t-shirt, white jeans, and sandals called huaraches that had car tires as the sole. Marty was black, six foot three, solid muscle, at Long Beach on a football scholarship. He had on gray gym shorts and a brown sweatshirt that said "49'er Football."

"A few minutes ago, a naked girl came to the door and wanted me to hide her out because somebody was chasing her and . . ." He trailed off at the looks on their faces. "Oh, yeah? She's still in the bedroom. Gentlemen, allow me to present . . ." He stopped because he realized he didn't know her name.

Of course, when Walt proudly led them into the bedroom and opened the hamper, it was empty.

Arlen did a Boris Karloff, or maybe it was supposed to be Igor, it was hard to tell—shuffling around the room, dragging one leg behind him—that was almost as bad as his surf talk. "I vas verking in ze lab late one night," he said, and Marty joined in with "When my eyes beheld an eerie sight." They were dancing around the bedroom, singing "The Monster Mash."

Walt said, "You guys cut class and went to the 49'er, didn't you?"

Arlen said sadly, "Life is short, man. You don't want to miss a chance at a schooner of beer. And we heard there was a pop quiz."

Marty threw his arm around Walt's shoulders. "Listen, I think maybe you've been spending too much time in the lab, you know? You need to get out some, get away from these, uh, comics. Hey, how about we go over to the quad for some Frisbee? Gotta stay in practice, man. We can take my car and check out where they found the dead guy." Walt was not a sports guy, but he could throw a Frisbee with the best of them.

"Dead guy?"

"Yesterday, on campus, man. Where have you been?"

Arlen nodded in agreement. "And you work all these crazy hours, man. I dreamed about a chick in a bikini last night. And she had stuff written on her like Goldie Hawn."

Marty said, "Is that a chicken joke?" They laughed. Then Marty turned serious. "Listen, man, those dreams are normal, you know?" He laughed again and clapped Arlen on the back, nearly knocking him off his feet.

And for one brief, horrible moment, Walter actually doubted. For Walter Dalrymple, the world divided into two parts: books that told him things he remembered, and people. The former made sense—Superman always wigged out when he was exposed to red Kryptonite just as fusion lit stars and powered the universe. People were black boxes. You never knew what to expect; they just did stuff. Penny, his ten-year-old sister, had coached him on what to say to a girl at a dance. He'd never actually said any of the things she'd taught him, but if the opportunity ever presented itself, he was ready.

They heard the toilet flush.

The girl in white boots came into the bedroom, modestly tugging down the sweatshirt. Arlen and Marty were speechless. Walt grinned and buffed his nails on his bare chest.

Arlen said, "She's wearing your sweatshirt."

She said, "Hi, guys. I'm Jane."

Arlen looked up at Marty and said again, "She's wearing his sweatshirt."

Arlen and Marty stared.

She repeated, "Hi, guys." Then she pointed at herself. "Me Jane. You . . ." She waited patiently.

"Marty. I'm Marty. Nice to meet you, Jane."

"Arlen. Uh, Arlen. Yeah, cool, nice to meet you." He looked at Marty and muttered, "No justice, man, no justice. Smartest kid in school and now this."

"Pleased to meet you both. Look, Walt, I have to go, but I need to talk to you first."

Walt shook his head. "We have to call the police."

Arlen promptly forgot his fascination with the fact that the girl was wearing his roommate's sweatshirt, which came down almost to mid-thigh, and said, "No cops, man. Are you nuts?"

Jane was looking at Walt. He sighed and said, "Look, there are two possible outcomes based on what Jane said being true."

Jane said, "It is true."

Marty shifted uncomfortably and said, "What's the problem?"

"Jane claims a girl was shot in the apartment above ours. The cops may be on their way. We can make the call and look honest, or we can try to run, get caught, and look guilty. I don't want to lose my scholarship."

"Shit! Shit! You don't care—you'll be off to Berkeley next year. You're really gonna call the pigs?" Arlen dashed into the room he shared with Marty. A moment later, he ran out, stuffing a Baggie down the front of his pants. "This is nothing. Not mine. Not mine, belongs to a friend. I have to go to the library. Big term paper. If the cops want to talk to me, I'll be back later. Big term paper. Library. Shit. Nice meeting you, uh . . ."

"Jane."

"Another body? You're not talking about the one they found on campus?" Jane shook her head. Marty shuffled his feet and said, "Man, I can't afford to get in trouble. Sorry, Walt, I gotta go too."

When Walt and Jane were alone again, he said, "There's really a dead girl upstairs?"

"Yes."

"Let's go take a look. I think that crazy guy's split."

"You don't trust me."

"I just think we should look."

She caught his arm. "Have you ever seen a dead body before? It's not pretty."

The Beachi Tiki apartments were built in a hollow square around a small, kidney-shaped pool. Exterior walkways circled the apartments on the second and third levels. Walt and Jane exited his apartment, turned right, and headed for the stairs. She said, "Call me Jane."

"Jane. I'm Walt."

"And you were working in the lab last night? Or are your roommates just, uh . . ."

"They're my friends. We went to high school together."

"They're kind of goofy."

"They're okay. Arlen wants to be a surfer. Marty's here on a football scholarship."

"What about the lab?"

"Yeah, I can get time on the equipment at midnight because nobody else wants it." They were at the door to the apartment directly above his. He looked at her, took a deep breath, and tried the handle. The door opened. They pushed in through strings of multi-colored plastic beads hanging from the top of the door to the floor.

The floor plan was like Walt's: a front door that opened into the living room; kitchen that was an alcove on the left, with room for a small table; two bedrooms, the master with bath. Short hall leading to two bedrooms.

It was a crashpad, an apartment where anybody could spend a few nights as long as they could kick in a little money for rent or some dope. The living room was crowded with two couches, a coffee table, two unrolled sleeping bags and a chest-high pyramid of beer cans constructed against one wall. Textbooks were piled on the coffee table and stacked next to both couches. With its orange and brown color scheme, and a sink in the kitchen that was more stained than white it looked almost normal for an apartment full of college kids, until Walt noticed that the phone in the kitchen had been ripped out of the wall. He quickly looked around the living room until he found the extension, a pink Princess phone, also ripped out of the wall and stomped on for good measure. There was a bad smell, faint, but unpleasant. The TV had rabbit ears with tinfoil cones on top, but the reception would be poor because the largest knob dangled down in front of the speaker on red and green wires. The cheap plastic stereo rested on top of a cinderblock-and-board bookcase, with an LP turning, stuck in a center groove. The tick, tick as the record turned was the only sound. Walt moved to turn the stereo off, but Jane put her hand on his arm and shook her head. The tick, tick went on.

Jane had not moved. She held his arm, watching him. She nodded toward the larger of the two bedrooms. The faint, unpleasant smell was coming from there. Tick, tick. Come on in. A car door slammed in the parking lot below, and he jumped. Jane let go of his arm. Tick, tick. Come on in.

He used his knuckle to push the bedroom door open.

And that's where he found her. She was lying on the carpet next to the bed, on her back, wearing a wraparound green plaid skirt held closed by a large gold safety pin in front, and a long-sleeved, fuzzy white sweater. The sweater had a gold circle virgin pin on it. The stocking on one leg was laddered, the other perfect. One of her penny loafers had come off and lay to the side. Her hair, what he could see of it, was light brown. Half of her face was gone, replaced by a red mass of flesh and white bone. Oddly, her hands were folded on her stomach, as if she had been laid out to rest carefully instead of shot and left to die.

Walt looked for a moment and then turned away. He stepped quickly into the bath and gripped the counter. Now he knew what the smell was. Once, in high school, one of the kids in biology had left a dissection specimen—an enormous green frog—out over a weekend. The apartment smelled like that—decomposition.

Okay, he could be sick later. Back in the living room, Jane was still standing by the door.

He said, "I have to go downstairs to call the cops."

"I'll wait here and make sure nobody goes in."

"Yeah, okay, that's good."

The phone in Walter's apartment had one of those stickers with emergency numbers on it. He wondered briefly who had put it on—certainly not the current residents or the previous dope dealers. Anything was better than thinking about the dead girl. Half her head was gone. Her hands were folded. And in the living room, the record on the stereo said tick, tick. He closed his eyes, took three deep breaths, and dialed.

After a surprisingly brief conversation, he agreed to meet the police outside the crashpad. When he went back upstairs, Jane was standing by the door. He managed a weak smile. "In the books, you'd be gone."

"What books?"

"You know, the Matt Helm books, or Shell Scott."

"Never heard of them."

At first, there was only one police car parked in the lot and visible from the crashpad's kitchen window, but that didn't last long—the first uniformed officer took one look at the body sprawled in blood and hustled down to his car and the radio, and in minutes, there was a crowd of two more black and whites, an ambulance, and a white Ford Econoline van labeled "Coroner." A moment later, an unmarked car pulled up behind the Econoline. Two men in suits got out.

The two plainclothes cops separated Walt and Jane to question them. They had Walt wait in the living room while they talked to Jane in the spare bedroom with the door closed. Then they repeated the process with Walt. He told them everything. When he came out, Jane was just pushing in through the beads hanging in the front door.

She said, "I think we're done for now."

She took his arm and guided him downstairs. Her arm was warm, and Walt wished they had a lot farther to walk; that is, he thought about her arm wrapped around his until he saw the door to his apartment standing open. They both stopped. He could hear voices behind them, from around the pool.

Jane frowned. "I thought you locked that."

"I did. I always do."

"Well, there's police all over the building, so I guess it's safe to go in."

Walt stood for a moment. "I always lock the door," he muttered. "My mother made me promise."

Jane let go of his arm and pushed the door all the way open with her boot. Inside, the apartment was a total wreck. The cushions were pulled off the couch, the drawers in the kitchen were open, and silverware was scattered over the counter and the floor. The bedrooms were worse. Walt's first thought was that he was glad Arlen had taken his stash with him.

Jane said, "Somebody was looking for something. And they were in a hurry,"

He could only nod. Then he said, "Cops." Once again, she waited by the door while he trooped upstairs and convinced a uniformed officer that his apartment had been trashed.

Downstairs, the officer looked at Jane. Then he looked around and said, "I seen other kids' places. This ain't so bad. Anything missing?"

"I don't think so."

"Okay. Look, kid, there's not much I can do, but I'll put it in the report."

After he left, Walt locked the door behind him and stood for a moment, resting his forehead against the wood. He wanted to think about his laser experiment, or Batman, or anything except girls with half their face gone and the stereo saying tick, tick.

A noise from the kitchen made him jump. When he caught his breath, he turned to see Jane picking up silverware and piling it into the dishwasher. Between the two of them, they restored the apartment to a semblance of order.

"Thanks again for the sweatshirt. I'll wash it and get it back to you."

"Yes, great, thanks. That would be nice."

"Walt..."

"Thanks."

"Thanks? I should be thanking you."

He managed a weak grin. The reality was sinking in, and what would he tell his parents? Would they make him move home? No, but what about his transfer to Berkeley? It didn't seem so attractive now, and he wasn't sure he wanted to go. "My roommates were pretty impressed. Hey, you got your purse."

"The cops let me pick it up while they were interviewing you." She kissed him on the cheek and left.

Walter Darlymple was eighteen, and before Jane had come to his door, the only naked women he'd ever seen had been in his cousin's *Playboys*. He hadn't exactly lied when he'd told Jane that he was a scientist; in many ways, he was one. He just didn't have the academic credentials yet. He had total recall for everything he had ever read or heard. He'd skipped two grades and graduated from Morningside High in Inglewood at sixteen, and a year later, he was doing actual research at Cal State Long Beach. In June, he was supposed to accept a scholarship and transfer to UC Berkeley, where the real cutting-edge stuff went on, experiments in coherent light that would remake the world. Light that could be bounced off the moon. He wondered if he should have tried to take her to bed, or at least make out. What if she had expected it and was disappointed in him? He wished he had his sister Penny to ask.

Later that afternoon, the police came back to the apartment building and asked other residents more questions. They didn't talk to Walter. He spent the afternoon packing his comics in boxes and putting them in the closet with his paperbacks—James Bond, Matt Helm, Shell Scott. He only knew the police were there because he'd seen the black and white in the parking lot when he'd gone down to get his bicycle. That night, he ran more experiments, working till dawn. Time on the equipment was valuable, and he was, after all, only a sophomore. The results were good. He made copious notes. And thought about blonde bangs over wide brown eyes. Then he peddled home on his three-speed.

He locked his bike up and hurried up the stairs to his apartment. Marty and Arlen were still asleep, so he entered quietly, went into his room, and closed the door. He changed into the black silk pajamas his parents had given him for his last birthday and lay on the bed, hands laced behind his head, and willed himself to sleep. When that didn't work, he got up and tried to read a chapter in *A Study of Matter and Energy*, but he found it impossible to focus. He paced. He went into the kitchen and made a cup of decaf Taster's Choice. Finally, he dozed on the couch for an hour, until his roommates got up and started cooking Pop-Tarts. They wolfed them down and left for class. He sat at the table and thought.

It didn't seem real. Could it be possible that less than twenty-four hours ago a half-naked girl had run into his apartment, and that he'd hidden her from a crazy man? No, it didn't seem possible, but he knew it had happened. He proved it by pulling his *Green Lantern* collection out of its storage box and looking at the one with the ripped cover. He shook his head. Wow. The other girl was dead. He wondered if anybody had taken the record off the stereo.

He said, "I give up. I have to see it," and pulled on jeans and a plain white t-shirt.

He couldn't shake the idea that he had missed something when he was in the crashpad, some piece of information that might be important. It made no sense. Walter did not like things that didn't make sense. In his world, equations balanced, gravity always accelerated a falling body at 32.2 feet/second^2, and unanswered questions were only waiting to be answered. So he found himself once again going up the stairs leading to the third floor and the scene of the murder.

A girl was sitting on the floor at the stairwell landing, her knees pulled up under her chin, her beaded purse next to her. The first words that popped into Walt's mind were *hippie chick*. She had light blue eyes, a round face, and thin blonde hair parted in the middle and hanging down past her shoulders, completely straight. She was wearing leather sandals, bellbottoms that had started life white but now were mottled with various stains, and a scoop-neck paisley long-sleeved blouse. From the way her heavy eyeliner had smeared, it looked like she'd been crying. He smiled half-heartedly and started to squeeze by. She grabbed his cuff and whispered, "Hey, man, you live upstairs?"

"Uh, no, I don't. Why do you ask?"

"I was staying there 'cause my old man was really wasted, and he was pissed 'cause I didn't make dinner, and I told him I had a big test, and that was bourgeoisie crap, and he got really pissed, so I came here, and I forgot my psych book. And now there's cops, and somebody said a girl got killed." She stopped this rush of words, took a breath, and got to her feet, hoisting her large beaded purse to her shoulder as she did. Standing next to Walt, she smelled of pot and patchouli.

"Yes, it's true. A girl named Becky was killed. Did you know her?"

"No! No way! I mean, I might have seen her, but I never talked to her, and my books are in there, and, like, I really need them, you know? Do you think they'd let me in? Are you going up there? What's your name? You don't talk much, do you?"

Two girls needing help in two days. Not possible. Not remotely possible. But here it was. "Let's find out about your books." As she brushed off the seat of her pants, he added, "I'm Walt."

"Needra. I'm Needra, but you know, everybody calls me Rabbit 'cause I'm always late and running for class, you know, like the White Rabbit."

"Pleased to meet you, Needra. So, which is it, book or books?"

"What?"

"First you said it was your Psych 101 book. Then you said 'books,' implying all of them." She gaped at him, displaying a set of braces on her teeth. He stopped halfway up the next set of stairs. "So, one book or all of them?"

She went on for a couple of steps and then turned and looked down at him. "All my books, they're all in there. But psych's the one I need most, 'cause we have a test and I think it might be open book." She stopped for breath again.

"Okay." Walt climbed to her level and they started up again.

"Wow. Two." She sounded stunned.

"Two?"

"You didn't hear? Yeah, they found a dead kid on campus, in that trench that goes up to *Hardfact*, and he was shot and everything, and I heard he might be, like SDS or something and the pigs murdered him." Her eyes were wide. As she told the last part, she kept looking around, making sure they were alone.

"Yes, I heard." Walt shook his head. "Needra, outside of movies, the police usually don't go around killing people."

"Shows how much you know, man. I bet there's lots of stuff the Establishment wants to keep from the people."

When they turned the corner and looked along the exterior walkway, they saw a uniformed cop standing in front of the crashpad. Needra clutched at Walt's arm. He had a brief flash of himself in a tuxedo with a cigarette, saying, "The lady is with me."

He explained that he was one of the people who had been interviewed after the body had been found, that he wanted to take a look around, and that this girl had left her textbooks in the apartment.

The cop, who didn't look like he was much older than they were, took off his dark glasses, inspected the lenses carefully, and said, "Yeah, okay. They're done in there, and they're taking the tape down in a little while. But I think I better stay with you."

They pushed through the beads and into the living room. Needra shot Walt a grateful look, gave his arm a squeeze, and began looking around. He grinned. *The lady is with me.* She started in the master bedroom, flinching at the bloodstains before carefully looking at a stack of books piled on the floor in the corner. She opened the closet and checked it. The young cop, who was dividing his time between trying to look down her top and keeping an eye on Walt, started growing visibly impatient. She looked under the bed and then stuck her head in the other bedroom for a quick look before returning to the living room. The stereo turntable had stopped. The arm was back on its rest. No tick, tick inviting them in. "Oh, look! Somebody moved them!" She picked up Psych150, Health 101, and half a dozen library books. "Wow, thanks, man, I really, really appreciate it." Her eyes darted around the place. "I never seen a place where somebody got murdered before. Did you see her? Was she, like, all bloody and stuff?"

"And if anybody asks, you haven't seen this one." Now that the hippie chick was done bending over, the cop had obviously reconsidered his kindness. He shooed them in the direction of the door. Walt stepped around him and returned to the site of the killing for a moment. He studied the room carefully, memorizing each detail. Later, when asked, he would say that was what they did in the books.

Outside, on the walkway overlooking the pool, Needra, also known as Rabbit, said again, "Thanks, man." She looked over her shoulder to make sure they were alone. "Hey, wanna smoke some grass? I got a couple joints."

"Sorry. I have to get to class."

She looked at her watch. "Oh shit, oh shit. Work! I gotta get to work too. I work in the library, in the circulation department and I was late last week, and my boss ragged on me right in front of everybody, and I gotta go. Thanks, man, far out, thanks." And she hurried away. He walked slowly back to his place and collected his books.

Half an hour later, he was locking his three-speed to a rack outside Science Building One, on the east side of campus. In later years, the buildings would undoubtedly be renamed after famous graduates or those who had donated large amounts of money, but the campus was barely twenty years old, so the three science building were named SC-1, SC-2, and SC-3. The buildings were on the east side of the large, grassy quad. The north end was torn up for construction of the Student Union. So far, the excavation was complete, blocked off by sawhorses and yellow tape that said, "Construction Site. Do Not Enter." The large hole was partially filled with stacks of lumber and bundles of rebar. Walt wanted to check the lab schedule to see if he could pick up some extra laser time before he went to the cafeteria for breakfast. After finding, as expected, that there was none available except the midnight-to-six-am time slot, he walked across the quad, heading for the cafeteria. He passed *Hardfact*, one of the massive sculptures built during a year-long sculpture symposium. It was a vertical, wedge-shaped black piece of metal standing at the end of a cement-lined trench that led up to it.

The crime scene tape from the murder was gone. A few daring kids had walked down into the cement trench.

As he approached the cafeteria, its walls covered with banners for Organization Day and the Spring Kick-Off Dance, with nothing more on his mind than a ham and cheese omelet, he noticed two men standing by the entrance. One was in his thirties, wearing a peach leisure suit over a green and red paisley shirt with long, drooping collars. The other was older, fifties maybe, wearing a blue suit, white shirt, and wide tie. Leisure Suit had a piece of paper in his hand, and as students walked in, he looked at it and then at the student. No, not all students, only boys. No, not only boys, only those with short hair.

Like Walt's.

Having a crazy man break into your apartment and push you around makes you paranoid. As Walt watched, a guy with a crew cut and a briefcase walked toward the doors. Leisure Suit stopped him, smiling, questioning. Words were exchanged, and the kid pulled out his wallet and showed ID. After Leisure Suit checked it, a few more words were exchanged, and the kid pushed through the double glass doors leading to the fraternity and sorority side of the cafeteria. The next kid was a tall, skinny hippie with love beads and Jesus waves down to his shoulders. He headed into the non-frat side and was not stopped.

Walt did stop. He moved to the side of the stream of kids moving up and down the hill. In 1970, Long Beach was bursting at the seams, with over thirty thousand students, full and part time. Walt moved casually back onto the grass and watched for a moment, and saw it happen again: briefcase = stop and question; long-haired freak = no questions. He thought that the odds of them being interested in him were astronomical, but he still watched. He had learned to play five-card draw at his father's knee, and that worthy, a CPA, had drilled him on gambling, and Rule #1 was Don't Make a Bet You Cannot Afford to Lose. No matter the odds, you must be prepared to pay up.

Walt didn't like to think about what might happen if he lost this particular bet. He had no idea what paying up might involve, but he knew he didn't want to find out.

He thought of three questions that needed answering. One, were they looking for him? If they were, why? And if they were looking for him, how much did they know about him?

He was walking south, on the far side of the stream of students, as he thought of a way to possibly answer two of the questions. His ten o'clock was a lecture class, Physics 101, and it was in LH 151, a hall that seated around two hundred. He veered off the main walk and took the stairs up to the second floor of the Liberal Arts building across from the lecture hall. The stairs were exterior, with a landing at the second level. It was a popular spot for a smoke before class, and the kids there cheerfully made room for him. One guy, an obvious frat rat, offered him a Tareyton, but he said no thanks and focused his attention on the entrance to the lecture hall. The crowd around the doors thinned as class time approached, eventually dwindling to a few, who hurried to the food machines across the patio for a cup of coffee to carry in.

At 9:55, the suits hustled up, standing out among the jeans and sweatshirts. Leisure Suit took up station by the food machines, where he could watch the door, while Blue Suit went inside. He came out a minute later and shook his head. He checked out the offerings in the machines and bought a donut and coffee. Walt turned away. The only way to learn more would be to walk up to the suits and say something like, "Hi, guys. Looking for me?" That was not appealing, so he made his way along the upper level and descended at the other end of the building.

Did they know about his bike, parked at SC-1? He had to assume they did. Now what? It wasn't that long a walk back to the Beachi Tiki apartments; he could be home in half an hour, but then what? *Proved: They know my class schedule. Assumption: They know where I live.*

The campus was relatively safe; if they tried to grab him he could yell for help and probably get it. Maybe he should approach them. He was actually considering it when he got lucky and had a better idea. Across the parking lot, heading north on State College Drive, he spotted a small truck, really a large golf cart with a small pickup bed in back, and he not only knew where it was going, he knew the driver.

Despite his age, he was often asked to tutor students who were struggling with calculus, and thus, he had met many more people than your average sophomore. Mikela, the girl driving the truck, was one of his first tutorees, and she always said if it hadn't been for him, she would have flunked, and she was right. He hurried down the stairs, sprinted across the parking lot, and flagged her down. Five minutes later, she was letting him off on Lower Campus, on the street fronting Campus Police. He had decided it was time to get some help. Those guys were certainly looking for him. Well, almost certainly— that "almost" in his mind slowed him as he walked through the parked cars toward the one-story, glass-fronted building. And that turned out to be a very good thing, because the nutcase he had nicknamed "Fireplug," the one who had ripped the cover of *Green Lantern* #29, was outside the building, leaning against a black Road Runner with serious body damage along the passenger side.

There was a moment when it didn't seem real, when his feet kept moving, carrying him out from the row of cars into plain sight. Then, all at once, it was real, and he stepped quickly back into hiding. Hysterical laughter almost bubbled up. He thought of going back to Upper Campus, finding the suits, and bringing them down here. He could introduce them—his mind skipped over the fact that he didn't know any of their names—and they could all go for pizza.

Bad idea, probably. They might want anchovies, and at that thought he felt hysterical laughter bubbling again.

It made him nuts that he had to say, "probably." He didn't *know* anything. He could run into Campus Police screaming, "Help, help, this guy's after me, and he wrecked a comic book, and he might be a killer." but the odds of Fireplug following him in were low, about the same as the campus cops really caring about *Green Lantern* #29. And as he watched, peering over the roof of a blue VW Beetle with flower decals pasted on the hood, he realized that he had another problem. The truck that had dropped him off was gone; Mikela was finishing her rounds of picking up books from remote book drops. If he walked back up the hill, he would be clearly visible to Fireplug. The only way to stay hidden was to go the other way and make his way through the parking lot down to Atherton Boulevard, and the walk home from there would be much longer.

And he didn't *want* to leave. So he settled in to see what would happen. Half an hour went by, and he was starting to feel the effects of the cup of Taster's Choice he'd had before leaving for school, when, all at once, Fireplug straightened and peered up the hill. He got into the car and pulled off to the side. Walt made a mental bet with himself and won when the suits trudged up. If they went into the police station, he'd run in after them. Instead, they got into a black sedan and drove away. Fireplug followed in the Road Runner. Okay, it looked like two sets of people were looking for him. The suits had his class schedule. Fireplug didn't seem to. But why had he staked out Campus Police? Was he waiting, not for Walt, but for the suits?

For the third time that day, he asked himself, "Now what?"

He was hungry, tired, and confused. The hell with it. He'd walk back to the science building, get his bike, and go home.

That thought changed as soon as the suits' sedan turned the corner, moving slowly, looking—for him. The other car was not in sight, but Walt was sure it was nearby. He ducked. Apparently, he hadn't been spotted. But they were after him, driving slowly up and down rows.

Staying low, he jogged in the direction of the dorms. The problem was, the dorms were at least a quarter-mile away, and he would be in plain sight at least once before he got there. A group of hippies walked by and piled into a VW van decorated with peace signs. Walt sprinted up to them.

"Hey, man, I need a ride bad. Can you take me out to Bellflower?"

The oldest person there, a girl who was at most twenty, said, "Who's after you?"

"I don't know, but they're following me."

"You holding?"

"No, no. No pot, nothing. I'm not crazy, really. It's two guys, older, wearing suits."

The girl looked at his short hair and scuffed briefcase. "Star?" A tiny Asian girl leaned forward from the back seat and stared at him intently, and the first girl said, "Star sees auras. If you're not cool, she'll know."

Star stared for another moment and then reached out and touched his cheek. "Let him in. Hurry."

When the sedan pulled in front of them and Leisure Suit got out, Walt was in the back of the van, under an unrolled sleeping bag, trying not to sneeze as dust went up his nose. He heard a voice say, "You see a kid with a briefcase? Short hair?"

"No, sir."

"We could search the car. Maybe we'd find something interesting."

Silence. Silence that dragged on. Walt slipped a hand up and pinched his nostrils shut.

"Okay, thanks. You kids behave."

"Yes, sir."

Footsteps moving away.

At last, Star whispered, "Where do you live?" Walt released his nostrils, pushed the sleeping bag away, and sneezed explosively.

Ten minutes later, having turned down a joint, a peyote button ("It's natural, man."), and a ride to a free concert, he was dropped off in front of the Beachi Tiki apartments. As he turned to slide the door shut, Star pressed his hand. "Peace, man."

"Uh, thanks."

Star nodded and released his hand.

Walt had been thinking about what to do when he got back to the apartment building, and he'd decided on a degree of caution, so instead of going straight upstairs, he went to the Manager's apartment on the first floor. Chuck Lorton was in his sixties, balding, with thin hair plastered across a bald spot and stained teeth. His main hobby was watching the girls sunbathe by the pool. If he'd had his way, the building would have rented only to co-eds, but he'd never succeeded at that.

"Mr. Lorton, can you let me into my apartment? I don't have my key."

Lorton dragged on his unfiltered Chesterfield and grunted. "Key replacement is five bucks."

"It's inside, I'm sure."

"You talked to the cops, didn't you?"

The old man hadn't moved, and Walt was getting nervous. He was standing in plain view, and sooner or later, one or more of the people after him would arrive.

"Please, I need to get in." *And I don't want to be by myself when I open the door.*

"You say your key's not lost? Just left it inside the apartment?"

"Right." He had an inspiration. "Let me in, and I'll tell you all about the murder. I saw the body and everything." Lorton's eyes lit up at the prospect of good gossip. He grunted and went to get his keys.

After the door was unlocked and the apartment shown to be empty, Walt gave the landlord a short version of his adventure, neglecting to mention the hole in the closet wall, and he sighed with relief when he was alone.

Once the door was locked, he sank down on the couch and tried to think. Normally, for Walter, thinking was easy; it was just what he did. But this was different. He needed advice. He very badly needed to talk to somebody.

He called home. He would tell his mother and father everything, and he wasn't sure what would come next. He listened as the phone rang in their Oceanside home. It was unusual that she'd be out in the middle of the morning, but as it rang for the tenth time—he had read somewhere that ten rings equaled a minute and that was an appropriate length of time to let the phone ring—he realized what she would say and do. She would have him lock himself in the apartment until his father could drive up and get him. He'd be on his way home in no time. And that made him hang up, grateful that there had been no answer.

There was a knock at the door. A cheery girl's voice said, "Pizza Girl. She delivers." And, when he opened the door, completely forgetting to look through the peephole, there she was, holding two cardboard boxes from Big John's, with a large macramé purse hanging off her shoulder. "Well, are you going to let me in?" She raised the boxes. They smelled wonderful, and he immediately realized he was starving. "I brought food. I wasn't sure if your roommates were home, so I brought two. One's pepperoni. The other's plain cheese." She was wearing a fuzzy green sweater, black leather miniskirt, and shiny black boots. She raised the pizza boxes so they were just under her wonderful eyes and kind of wiggled the boxes back and forth. "Pizza. See?"

He was practically dumbstruck. All he could think was: *She kissed me. This girl kissed me, and it was a real kiss.* "Um, sure, come in. Pizza?"

"And your shirt. I brought your sweatshirt. Let's eat. I'm starved."

He nodded. If she had suggested that he take off all his clothes, paint his privates blue, and run down the middle of the 405 freeway, Walter would have nodded.

In addition to the trick clothes hamper, the previous tenants had appropriated a huge wooden spool previously used for telephone cable, sanded it, and stained it dark brown. When they'd abruptly left, escorted out in handcuffs, the table had stayed. Walt got out paper plates and a roll of paper towels, and they settled in. Sitting at the table, elbows propped comfortably, she abruptly said, "Thank you," and looked down as she tugged a slice of cheese pizza free.

Walter blushed. She put her hand over his. It was soft and warm and perfect, just like her eyes; they were perfect too. "I was getting ready for class, and he was there with a gun. He shot Becky, and I ran, but he came back. I saw his car pull in, and I knew what he'd done, and so I just freaked, you know, just ran and pounded on your door." His blush deepened, and he was thankful he was sitting down. "You were really great about it And boy, that was quick thinking, the way you hid me." She wiped her fingers on a paper towel and squeezed his hand before reaching into her bag and pulling out his shirt. "Here's your sweatshirt, all washed and everything." She set it on the table. Then she picked up her pizza and took a bite.

He said, "I, uh, yeah, no, good, good pizza. We go to Big John's all the time. Shoot pool and, you know, hang out, pick up girls, and—"

"Yeah, it's great."

He blurted out, "I've never been there."

She ducked her head to catch the end of a new slice of pizza as it drooped. "Been where?"

Now he was blushing furiously, and his hands shook as he put his untasted slice of pizza down. "Big, Big John's. I was going to go once with some guys from the dorm, but they left without me, and I heard they got in a fight anyway."

"Okay. Why did you make up a story?"

"You mean lie. I just wanted to impress you, you know, so you wouldn't think I-I don't know." *That was lame.*

She took another bite, chewed thoughtfully, and dabbed at her lips with a napkin, leaving a spot of hot pink lipstick behind. "Okay, sure. Then why did you change your mind and tell the truth?"

"I don't know that either, except I didn't want to lie to you."

"Do you have anything to drink? Coke? Pepsi?"

Keeping his back to her as much as possible, he got up and got two cans of Tab from the refrigerator, and glasses that Arlen had collected for filling up his car at a gas station on Atherton. She pulled off the top and dropped it inside the can, poured, had a sip, and went on.

"Eat your pizza, Walter. So, what do you do in the lab at night? I think that was supposed to be the 'Monster Mash' your roommates were doing."

"They can be real spazzes sometimes. Uh, in the lab, I work with the laser. Time on it is hard to get, and I'm only a sophomore, so I work mostly at night."

"Laser?"

"Coherent light. Regular light is a lot of wavelengths; a laser produces a beam that's just one. It stands for Light Amplification by Stimulated Emissions of Radiation, and . . ." He trailed off.

To his surprise, she said, "Wow, that sounds interesting. Maybe sometime I could come up and you could show me how it works."

"Well, there's not much to see, I mean, I don't, I'm just doing light experiments, but I mean, yes, of course, great, I'll show you all around; the lab is really neat . . ."

She smiled. "And yes, I'd love to."

"You would? Come to the lab?"

"That too. Yes, Walter, I would love to."

"Wow. Uh, you mean, uh, what? What do you mean?"

"The Spring Kick Off Dance. Cafeteria, bands, wild arm waving, you know."

He could only stare.

She snapped her fingers in front of his face. "Hello? Earth to Walter. Dance? Frug? Watusi? Do the Swim? You dance, right?"

"Of course. Sure. I go to dances all the time." He'd actually gone to the Welcome Frosh dance last year. It had been free, and so he'd ridden his bike up to the cafeteria and watched for a while. His roommates had been out, and for the first time in his life, Walter had been alone. No brother to play Monopoly or watch TV with. No little sister to help with her homework. He hadn't minded being alone, but the dance had been something to do after reading all day.

"I saw the flyer on your coffee table."

He thought: *Did I hear that right? She wants to go to the dance? With me?* He could only nod. And nod. And blush. Then he had a terrible thought, but before he could decide how to phrase it—maybe "I'll meet you there"—she said, "We can take my car if you want." He could only nod. And nod. And blush. Walter had passed driver training by promising the teacher that he would practice a lot before he started driving for real. At present, his Huffy three-speed was his only mode of transportation.

They ate pizza in silence for a while. Then she stood and, after rinsing her hands in the sink, found Arlen's favorite album—Dick Dale's *Surfer's Choice.* She put it on the stereo, took Walter's hand, and pulled him to his feet. "The dances here may be a little different than the ones you did back home. This is the Swim." She wiggled around as the twangy surf guitar blared from the stereo in "Surf Beat," pushing her arms out in front of her in an imitation breaststroke. Walt thought he'd probably died and gone to heaven.

"Now you." So, they tried it, and to his surprise, he wasn't awful. He even got the part where you hold your nose with one hand, wave the other over your head, and pretend to be going down. And it was as much fun as he imagined it would be—no, it was even better. It was *great.* Then it got even better as she found another album and put on a slow song, exactly the kind of song that had forced him even farther back toward the wall in the high school gym while the couples, kids that were going steady, took over the floor. He stood awkwardly, sort of holding out his arms. Jane took one hand and placed it at her waist, folded her fingers through the other, and, as Percy Faith's "Theme From A Summer Place" played, rested her chin on his shoulder, and they danced. She was warm and soft and seemed to have no bones in her body. Her blonde hair, sprayed into a flip, tickled his nose. Walt decided dancing was something he could get used to. "When we dance slow, you guide me around with pressure from the hand on my waist. That's how I know what to do." A moment later, she murmured, "You're glad to see me," and he wanted to fall through the floor, but she just giggled and continued to press against him.

Jane lifted her arm and looked at her watch over his shoulder. "You got it, Walt. You're not ready for *Bandstand,* but you can officially dance. Now I gotta go."

All at once, he remembered. The morning's chase came back to him in detail.

"Wait. Jane, I need to talk to you. It's important, I think. Some very weird stuff happened today."

She looked at him and nodded. They sat back down at the spool table, and he told her about the appearance of the suits outside the cafeteria and outside LH-151, of his stakeout at the campus police station, and his escape with the vanload of hippies. To his surprise, she didn't say he was paranoid or overreacting. Instead, she pursed her lips and looked at him grimly as he finished by saying, "But it's okay. I got away. We can still go to the dance, right?"

"Two strange men and one known crazy tried to follow you around campus, and your biggest concern is whether we can still go to the Spring Kick-Off?"

"Um, well, yes."

She just shook her head. "Outside Campus Police, you're sure it was the guy who crashed into your apartment? The one who shot Becky?"

"Yes. It was him. I thought he was after me, but that made no sense, and then he followed the other guys."

"The other guys," she mused. "Okay. You need to stay away from him. He's dangerous."

"Wow, he was nuts, totally batshit. Who is he?"

"His name is Morovich, first name Hubert, but God help the poor fool who calls him that." She seemed to decide something. "I'm not sure about the other two. I think you'll be all right. Whatever he's looking for, you don't have." She looked at him intently as she said it. "He's just a guy who showed up at the crashpad about two weeks ago. A little old, but he always had good shit. He knew Becky." She paused and then reached out and took his hand. "Listen, Walter, the way you stood up to Morovich was great, but you need to stay away from him in the future, okay? I mean it. If you see him coming, you go the other way."

"What's he after?"

"The last time I saw him, he was holding a gun and telling me to take it off."

"Before you came to the door." Walter grinned. "I'm glad Arlen and Marty came home. They wouldn't have believed me without witnesses."

"Okay, I'll see you Friday."

"Great, great."

She opened her purse, pulled out a mirror and lipstick, and applied it. Walter thought it was the sexiest thing he'd ever seen. She put the lipstick back in a little case and stowed it in the purse, stood, and smiled. "I have to go to class now. I had a nice time."

He jumped to his feet. "Oh. Uh, thanks for lunch. The pizza was great; I really like pizza. And you got pepperoni, my favorite. Is pepperoni your favorite too?"

"I don't think I've ever met a pizza I didn't like." She slipped her arm through his, and they walked to the door. "So, have the police been here? After the first time?"

"Yes, two plainclothes officers, but only for a brief time. It was perfunctory, and they only talked to other people, not me. That guy Morovich is crazy."

"No kidding."

He waited a moment to see what else she might say. Finally, he said, "Makes Norman Bates look sane."

"Oh, yes." She thought a moment and then pulled a pen and a notepad out of her purse. "Here's my number. Call me if the police come back. I'd like to know what they ask. And if you see Morovich again, call me at once. Doesn't matter if it's late, okay?" She handed him the paper.

They were standing at his door. She faced him a moment and then took him by the shoulders and kissed him firmly. She said. "Better wipe that lipstick off before the guys come back." She grinned. "Or not."

He blurted out, "I'll walk you to your car."

She smiled a slow smile and slipped her arm through his. "That would be nice."

He locked the door before they walked downstairs to where she had parked her odd-looking vehicle. It seemed to have small fins sticking out of the back at a thirty-degree angle, and various bulges and swoops in the sheet metal. "Walt, meet Prince. Prince, this is Walter Dalrymple."

Comics veteran that he was, Walt said at once, "He's a Valiant."

He opened the door, and she slid in, flashing him a quick glimpse of stocking-clad legs. She pulled him close and gave him another quick kiss.

Walt wasn't sure how he got back upstairs, but he thought he probably levitated. Or maybe he zoomed up like Sean Connery in *Thunderball* with his jetpack.

He did remember to lock the door behind him before wrapping the leftover pizza in tinfoil. Then he fell asleep on the couch, thinking about blonde hair in a flip and warm brown eyes. She had lied about what the crazy guy was looking for. He didn't care, at least not much. He had a date for the dance. All at once, he sat up, grabbed his lab book, and made a shopping list. Three boxes of Tic Tacs were the number one item. Matches. He should take some in case she smoked. He thought of one other item, but he knew there was no hope, and he didn't know where to buy them; he thought maybe a drugstore. What if the man behind the counter asked what size? And what if it was a girl behind the counter? If his older brother weren't off at basic training, Walt could've asked him.

He was so ecstatic that when there was a knock at the door, he opened it, thinking it must be Jane coming back to tell him something, like maybe what Morovich was looking for.

Bad Suit pushed his way in, followed by Leisure Suit. Leisure Suit whispered, "Walter Dalrymple? Thank goodness! We've been looking for you." Then he held a finger to his lips and gestured at his partner. Bad Suit quickly went through the apartment, checking all the rooms. A minute later, he came back and said, "Clear."

The young one gently closed the door and turned the deadbolt. "My name is Leonard Minkoff. My friend is Stanley Thibert."

Walt was slowly backing toward the kitchen. There was at least one sharp knife in the drawer. Or was it in the dishwasher? It was Marty's turn in the kitchen, and he was sometimes on top of it, sometimes not. When the football team was doing two-a-days, it knocked him out.

"Sit, please. We need to talk to you," Leisure Suit – Minkoff – gestured at the couch. Bad suit -- Thibert went into the kitchen.

Walt perched on the arm of the couch. "Listen, my roommates will be back any minute, and Marty's bringing some of the football team over, so you better leave."

"We know about what happened yesterday, the dead girl upstairs and the blonde that came to your apartment. We're looking for her."

"Are you guys cops?"

"Us? No, no. We're bookkeepers." Walt's jaw must have dropped. "Really, we are. The girl that got killed stole some stuff from the company we work for, and if we don't get it back we're in deep shit."

From the kitchen, Thibert said, "Deep shit. Right." His voice was odd, muffled. He came out holding a slice of pizza with a bite missing. "Hey, can I have this? I'm starved."

Walt could only nod. "What about the crazy guy who broke in looking for her?"

Minkoff sat on the couch next to Walt and looked him in the eye. "His name's Morovich, and he's crazy. You want to stay away from him." All the parties involved seemed to agree on that. "He was partners with the dead girl."

"Her name was Becky."

"Yeah, right, kid. Rebecca Darden. Well, they stole something. We sort of screwed up, see, so we have to get it back."

"What is it she stole?"

"Can't tell you that."

"Then I can't help you, can I?"

"Don't get smart with us, kid."

Walt very rarely got mad, but when he did, it was over the top. He stood. "Don't get smart? Listen, I was in my own apartment, asleep, when people started barging in and making threats. I saw you two on campus, obviously looking for me. And I saw the crazy guy, Morovich, following you."

Minkoff paled. "You sure? Kid, are you sure it was him?"

"Yeah, and you never knew he was there, did you? So, you need to tell me what you're looking for, or you need to get out. I mean it. I'm done with this."

They looked at each other. Finally, Thibert jammed the pizza crust into his mouth and said, "A notebook. Darden stole a notebook with important information in it. Morovich wants it. We need to get it back, all right?"

Walt said, "What's in the notebook?"

Minkoff answered, "We don't know, not exactly."

"What do you *think* is in the notebook?"

He shook his head and said, "For your own good, tell us where it is."

"I haven't seen it. I think I met the dead girl once or twice, down at the mailboxes, but that's all. If I hear anything, I could call. What's your office number?"

Minkoff quickly said, "Our Signal Hill office is closed. Don't worry, we'll be in touch."

At the door, Thibert said, "Thanks for the pizza. Listen, kid, I can tell you're okay, not one of them hippies. You need to level with us."

"I have."

"Right, I guess I believe you. Okay, listen, we gotta go. Remember, we're the good guys, really."

"Got it. You're the good guys."

Walt started to close the door. Thibert pushed it open and stuck his head in. "And stay away from Morovich. He's dangerous."

Walt locked the door behind them.

He boiled water and made a cup of Taster's Choice. Then he sat on the couch and thought. And since thinking was one of the things that Walter Dalrymple did best, he reached conclusions very quickly.

First, he was glad no one had answered when he had tried to call his parents. They would make him come home. And in truth, that might be the smart thing to do. He could go to the police, but they were already involved. He could tell them about the two "bookkeepers," but the most that would happen would be the cops questioning them, if they even tried to find them.

That evening, he got a ride to school with a kid from a ground-floor apartment who wanted to hear about the killing. He spent the night working on his experiments, carefully recording the results and not thinking about any of the strange people invading his life. He did think about white boots and arms crossed over breasts, a lot, and, after carefully checking in the small classroom attached to the lab to make sure it was empty, he practiced the swim while he waited for the magnets to cycle.

The last run finished, he shut off the equipment and locked the basement lab, he trudged up the stairs to the ground floor and walked over to the cafeteria, where he caught a ride back to the apartment and fell asleep.

Noise from the crashpad woke him up. Exhausted both by the events and by lack of sleep, he drank a glass of warm milk and went back to bed. Around two, he got up and made it to his three o'clock. Thibert and Minkoff were sitting on the cement benches outside SC-I, sipping paper cups of machine coffee, Minkoff in another leisure suit, Thibert in the same blue suit. Thibert set down his coffee and carefully extracted a food-machine donut out of its plastic wrapper. They didn't speak as Walt hurried by.

There was no sign of Morovich.

After the lecture, Walt went back to his apartment and spent the evening reviewing and collating results. His experiments had reached a point where he needed time to tabulate and assemble data, so he gave up his lab time.

The next morning, he was awakened again by pounding from the apartment above and feet going up and down the stairs. Still exhausted, grainy-eyed from lack of sleep, but driven by a scientist's obsession to *know*, he stumbled upstairs to stand outside the door and watch. The chocolate-brown shag carpet was on the landing, rolled up and ready to be carried downstairs. He could hear the sound of water running and cheerful Spanish from inside the apartment. A couple of kids he knew by sight as residents were in the hall watching. Needra trotted by in a paisley ankle-length dress, with multiple strands of love beads around her neck and at least a half-dozen bracelets on each wrist, and said, "Hi, Walt. I'm late, but thanks for getting my books. Thanks, man, I gotta go 'cause I'm late." She flashed the peace sign at him. He grinned and waved as she hurried off, her ears sticking out of her thin blonde hair, her bracelets and beads rattling.

There was a stack of a dozen books on the floor next to the door, all with call numbers. A uniformed cop came out and saw Walt looking at them.

"The victim—"

"Becky. Her name was Becky."

"Yeah. She had a lot of library books. I remember you. You were the one who called it in. Found the body." The cop was standing close enough for Walt to catch a whiff of his aftershave, and after a moment, he recognized it as Hai Karate, Arlen's favorite brand because he loved the commercials.

"Yes, well, not exactly. A girl came to my door, and then we came upstairs and found the body. I mean, we found Becky." Somehow it seemed better, more respectful, to use her name. "What about the books?"

"Well, somebody decided they're not evidence, so somebody needs to take 'em back to the library."

"I can do that."

"Really?"

"No problem. I have to go up there anyway. Listen, I saw the guy that broke into my apartment. He was on campus yesterday."

"Hmm. Did he threaten you in any way?"

"No. Well, he's a scary guy. I think his name might be Morovich."

The cop paused. "Okay, I'll pass the info on to the detectives. Thanks for dealing with the library books." That was so clearly a dismissal that even Walt got it. The cop stopped him after he picked up the books and said, "Listen, kid, this is a murder investigation. It would be better if you didn't discuss it with anybody, especially what might be the name of the guy, okay?"

Walt started to say something like "Everybody knows his name," but the uniform had turned away to move the spectators back as two Hispanic men hoisted the carpet roll with a grunt and maneuvered it down the stairs.

Back in his apartment, Walt put the library books on the table and looked at them. He opened a can of Tab and poured it into one of Arlen's gas-station glasses. He still wasn't satisfied. One of the detectives who had interviewed him had given him a card with his desk extension on it. Walt called the number, but before he could launch into his story, the detective said, "Yeah, kid, the uniform called it in. There's not much we can do unless this guy comes back, you know? But thanks for calling. Be sure and let us know if he shows up."

"But—"

"Thanks for calling." The line went dead.

Walt sat on the couch for several minutes, drinking the cola and thinking. He looked at the books. Becky had evidently used one of her registration cards, keypunched so it could be machine-processed, as a bookmark because it was sticking out of a book. He pulled it out and stared at it curiously.

Rebecca Q. Darden. Social Security Number. Literature. 150B. English Literature 1500—Modern. He wondered if she had liked the classes, if she had done the term papers. But she had scrawled "PS I Love You" in orange highlighter across the back of the card. *Well, well. A remarkable coincidence? Sure.* He carefully went through all the other books and found nothing. On a hunch, he opened his briefcase and slipped the registration card into the pocket. Now that he had the books stacked on the spool table, he realized that it would be difficult to carry them all on his bike. That was okay, since he had a Plan B. He groped in his cords and pulled out the piece of paper with Jane's number on it and called. There was no answer, so he spent a fruitless half-hour flipping through Becky's books, looking for anything. Maybe he'd find a note, written in blood of course, saying "Morovich killed me and here's his address." The cops would listen to him then.

He finished and called Jane again. This time, she answered. He heard her voice and imagined the lips behind it and was tongue-tied for a moment. What if she hadn't meant any of it? The kiss, the dance, it was all some kind of joke.

She said, "Hello. I know you're there. Okay, I give up. Good—"

"Wait! Jane, it's me, Walt, from the apartment and—"

"Walt, I know who you are. I'm glad you called."

"Uh, why?" Boy, that came out wrong. Shell Scott would know what to say.

"It's good to talk to you, silly. I meant to tell you to practice your Watusi before we go to the dance. You don't look like a native." She paused. Walt was stuck. He couldn't think of a thing to say except he was sorry and he'd try to dance better. "That was a joke, you goof."

"Oh. Good one, yeah. Native. I get it. I'm a white guy." Then he blurted out, "You'll still go to the dance with me?"

"Of *course.* Well, three Sigma Sigmas asked me, but I told them I had a date."

"You did?"

"Joke, Walt. Joke. Did you call just to chat?"

Walt had never called anyone, let alone a pretty girl, in his entire life "just to chat." In fact, he couldn't think of a time he'd ever chatted, and now he knew why. It was hard and not particularly fun. He blurted out, "I need to talk to you."

"Okay, talk."

"No, I mean in person."

"Why, Walter, are you asking me out on a date?"

"No, no, I—"

"Walt, Walt, you need to get out from behind the test tubes."

"I'm studying physics, lasers. We don't use many test tubes, and—"

"Here's a lesson: when a young lady says, 'Are you asking me on a date,' the answer is *always* yes." He didn't need to look in his wallet to know that he had eight dollars to last until his next check from his parents, and tutoring checks only came once a month. "But let's keep it simple. I've eaten, so let's just go for coffee. And I need feed Prince some gas anyway, so I'll pick you up. Make it about half an hour, in the parking lot."

"Thirty minutes. Parking lot. The one behind my apartment building, right? The gas station on Atherton behind the school gives you a free water glass if you fill up but it has to be over ten gallons. And when you turn into the parking lot at the apartment there's a bad speed bump . . ."

"Far out. See you then."

So, ten minutes later, he was standing in the parking lot behind the Beachi Tiki, with Becky's books stacked neatly on the pavement in front of him. It was almost sunset when Prince, rolled in and pulled into an empty space next to him. He picked up the books, hurried to the driver's window, and blurted, "I can explain. I just need to put these in a book drop. It's not far out of your way, really."

"Hi, Walt." She grinned. "Sure, no problem. Let's put them in the trunk." He stepped back, and she got out—he was a little disappointed that the skirt had been replaced by white pedal pushers and a brown sweatshirt—and opened the trunk, and at that moment, the black Road Runner bounced over the speed bump and slid to a stop behind the Valiant. As Walt gaped, the books in his arms forgotten, Morovich leapt out, threw open the Road Runner's trunk, grabbed Jane around the waist, and lifted her off the ground. She yelled, "Run, Walt, run!" Dropping the books, Walt ran—straight at Morovich. The fireplug had one arm around Jane's waist; with the other, he casually straight-armed Walt in the shoulder. He staggered back, caught Prince's tailfin, and managed to keep his feet. When he looked up, Morovich had stuffed Jane in the trunk. He slammed the lid and jumped behind the wheel, and the big black car made a k-turn before it vanished into the southbound traffic on Bellflower. For a moment, Walt was paralyzed, standing next to the pile of books with his mouth open, then he jumped in the Valiant's driver's seat and reached for the keys.

Unfortunately, Jane must have taken them out to unlock Prince's trunk; anyway, the keys with the rainbow peace symbol were not in the ignition. *Sure, she pulled them out to unlock the trunk.* He jumped out and searched the blacktop around the rear of the car. Finding nothing except a scrap of paper, he gave one of the tires a good kick and tried to think. Then he looked at the scrap of paper in his hand and saw that it was a blurry carbon copy of a receipt for rental on a boat slip in the downtown marina across from the old Queen Mary ocean liner, now under conversion to a luxury hotel. Walt thought a moment, grinned, and quit looking for Prince's keys. He scooped up the pile of books and tossed them into Prince's back seat.

Minutes later, he was on his three-speed, pedaling down Bellflower and then through the traffic on Second Street, heavy traffic that worked in his favor since he could ride on the extreme right or, if necessary, on the sidewalk. It actually seemed like it would work—once he caught a glimpse of the Road Runner as it crested the first bridge leading over a channel that on the way to Belmont Shore, a part of Long Beach centered on Second Street that was composed of small post-war houses and apartment buildings.

He followed Second Street to Ocean Boulevard and a few minutes later he was threading his way through a parking lot. He had never been to the marina before and was baffled at first by the size and complexity. Standing on the pedals and coasting, he could see that the parking lot was easily a half-mile long, with twelve rows of spaces, mostly full. He stopped himself when he started estimating the number of cars it contained, straddled the bike and thought. Setting sun, Queen Mary, water, and boats on his left, shops and restaurants on his right. Then he nodded and rode toward the water, ignoring cars, reading signs, and in the dying light it wasn't too hard to spot the one he was looking for.

Boat Owners Parking.

And there it was, the black Road Runner, complete with "Beep Beep" decal and scrape along the driver's side. He looked it over from a distance, then approached cautiously. Without getting off the bike reached out and tapped on the trunk lid. On the second tap it swung open. Empty. As he expected. He studied the situation, shading his eyes against the afternoon sun. There was a bike path, then a grass border, and then a steep, rock-covered slope leading down to the water and the docks full of boats—sailboats, cabin cruisers, big speedboats with outboard motors hanging off the back—all bobbing gently. Sliding to a stop, he saw his next problem. The ramps leading down to the docks were behind locked gates. Of course there was no sign of Jane or Morovich. All he could see to do was pedal his bike along the path that ran along the shore. He made one trip and was on the return leg when he got lucky. One of the gates was open. The dock it led to was about six feet wide, with narrow fingers sticking out at right angles between the boats.

He briefly considered hiding the three-speed, then decided he wanted it close, threw it down on the grass and hurried to the gate. Pushed it open, and stood just outside for a moment, assessing. He had no way of knowing if this was the right dock or of identifying the boat Jane was captive on, and if he found it, he wasn't sure what he would do. Challenge Morovich to a fist fight? Walt liked to have a plan, to know where he was going and what he would do when he got there, but in this case, the plan seemed to involve Morovich pounding him into jelly and not helping Jane.

In the fading light, he pushed the gate all the way open, went back to the bordering rock slope, and picked up one of the smaller rocks, a smooth, round one about the size of a baseball. He clutched it in his hand as he crept along the dock, past boats that were all locked and dark. Then, two floating dock fingers away, a light came on in one of the boats.

Stepping carefully to avoid rocking the dock, he crept toward the lighted boat. On the side, it said, "Chris Craft," which he assumed was the name of the manufacturer. On the stern in elaborate gold script it said, "Fish Finder," which was probably the name of the boat. The slip next to Fish Finder was empty. As he got closer he could hear raised voices.

Morovich said, "Listen, you know what happens if I don't find it."

Jane said, "We can work it out. Swear to God."

There was a wooden stepstool next to the stern of Fish Finder. Walt tentatively climbed up and clutching his rock, stepped awkwardly over the lifelines and into the area at the rear of the boat that had seating all around the border. He thought that, probably, when the boat was in use, there were cushions, but now the seats were only bare white fiberglass. *So far so good.*

All at once, Morovich launched himself up out of the cabin, arms spread, trying to tackle Walt, but he jumped up on the seat, and Morovich missed, landing with a grunt in the center footwell, wedging himself into the narrow space.

Walt, who remembered every playground assault where he'd lost lunch money, dignity, or both, didn't hesitate. As the fireplug heaved himself to his feet, Walt stepped up and hit him in the stomach as hard as he could with the fist holding the baseball-sized rock. The results were everything he hoped for. The fireplug's eyes widened and he doubled over, holding his midsection and making gagging noises before sinking to his knees, this time all the way down in the footwell. Walt began to worry that he'd seriously injured the guy; however, concerns about possible ruptured spleens receded into the background when Jane climbed out of the cabin, stepped over Morovich, and started hugging Walt, and all concerns vanished completely when she kissed him enthusiastically. He dropped the rock, got one arm around her waist, and steadied them by clutching the lifeline. Still clinging to him, she maneuvered them off the boat and down onto the dock.

"I knew you'd come," she gasped. "I just knew it."

She started to say something else when, all at once, Morovich was there, flying over the lifeline and tackling them both. They all went off the dock into the water.

Suddenly it was chaos. Walt lost track of Jane as the sea closed over his head. He flailed for the surface, couldn't find it, and then flailed some more, rising only to find slimy wooden planks between him and air. *I'm under the dock. I'm under the boat. No, I'm under either the main wide dock or the little ones, and I can't breathe. And I'm running out of air. Morovich jumped off the boat and knocked us into the water—into the empty slip next to Fish Finder. I didn't have time to suck in a breath, so I can't breathe. I can't breathe!* The rough underside of the dock seemed to go on forever.

If I pass out, my body will either sink, or be trapped under the dock, and it won't matter which because they won't find me. Decomposition creates gasses, so my corpse will bloat and rise to the surface and eventually be found. I'll smell like that frog that got left out in the lab. Tick, tick. Come on in. See the dead boy. The urge to open his mouth and suck in anything, even seawater, was almost too strong to resist.

I can't breathe!

I can't thrash; I only have time to go one way. And it's dark.

He opened his eyes.

The saltwater burned, burned. It hurt, hurt, but yes, there was light, light shining on the surface. That way.

Involuntarily he closed his burning eyes again and groped along the underside of the dock, listening to whimpering—his whimpering—as he clamped his jaws shut. Suddenly his fingers felt a smooth surface, maybe rubber? He realized he was touching the cylindrical plastic thing that hung between the boat and the dock, and that meant he was under the narrow finger not the main dock. There wasn't room between boat and dock for him to get his face up, so he had to go back, clawing at the wood, digging with his nails.

As panic started to overwhelm him, he groped along the planks, hoping that he could find the edge, until, at last, one hand was pushing against barnacles and nasty sea growth, but the other broke the surface. He followed it and pushed his face up, gasping for breath, with burning eyes, clothes that were pulling him down, and no idea where Jane or Morovich were.

"Walt, here." Jane was there, locking his neck in the crook of her elbow in the approved life-saver position and dragging him toward the rocky shore.

He spluttered, "I can swim."

"Okay." She let go of his neck.

He could hear splashes behind them. "Is that him?"

"Yeah. Quiet."

In a moment, his feet touched something slippery, and they clambered out on the rocky sloping hill that bordered the bike path. Jane whispered again, "Be quiet." They began to climb up.

"I'll find you, bitch. You know I will." The angry voice was accompanied by splashes as Morovich flailed. "All right! Go ahead, run! You got forty-eight hours. After that, it gets ugly."

"Come on." She led Walt up to the bike path and into the parking lot. "How did you get here?"

"Bike."

"You drive a motorcycle?"

"Three-speed."

"Oh."

"In Belmont Shore traffic, it's easier to catch a car on a bike."

"Okay, where's your bike?"

"Right there." He hurried over and picked it up. "We can ride double." He'd never had another person on the back, but how hard could it be? He'd seen lots of kids do it.

"Did you see where Morovich parked?"

"Over there." Walt pointed.

"We'll take his car. I saw him leave the keys in it. Come on, bring the bike."

They ran over to the big black car, and sure enough, the keys were in the ignition. Jane opened the trunk, and Walt lifted the Huffy and put it in. Jane produced a length of rope and tied down the trunk lid. In the distance, they could hear Morovich shouting something unintelligible. It didn't sound friendly, something like "rip your fucking lungs out and eat them."

Jane drove, slamming the big car through lanes at every opportunity, pushing her dripping bangs out of her face. She said, "We need a safe place to talk. How about this lab of yours?"

"I don't have the laser till midnight. But I have an idea, someplace he won't look. And it will do us some good."

"All right. Lab later. What now?" She turned onto Second Street.

He grinned. "Well, it's not laundry night." An idea was beginning to form in the back of his mind. "We have a little while since we've got his car. We'll go to my place and get laundry and then go to a laundromat I use."

She stopped at a red light in front of Big John's Pizza and Pool and shook her head. "You're crazy, you know that?"

The light changed, and the traffic inched forward. "No, really, it will work, I think. I never do laundry on Wednesday; *Hawaii Five-O*'s on. I'm not crazy."

"Well, it's certainly something he won't expect. But we've got to be quick because, once he gets out of the water and finds his car gone, he'll get another and come after us. If we're lucky, he'll stop to put on dry clothes."

"I didn't like that lung-ripping talk."

"Try not to think about it." She grinned and seemed to relax a little.

At the Beachi Tiki she put the Road Runner in a guest spot, and they got out. Jane started to say, "I'll leave the keys on the seat," when a dark figure rushed out of the shadows and ran at them, yelling something.

Jane rolled the figure over her shoulder and onto the ground. The fight, if there was any, went out of the attacker.

Walt decided he might be crazy after all, restrained in some pleasant, sunny room with padded walls and muscular, smiling orderlies.

He said, "Mom?"

For several minutes, there was total confusion, all of them talking at once.

"This is your mother?"

"Walter, are you all right?"

"Are you all right, Mom?"

"This is your *mother*?"

Gradually they stopped. Walt's mother gasped, "Walter Dalrymple, you're soaking wet. Why are you all wet? You'll catch your death."

"Mom, I can explain. Uh, Mom, this is Jane. Jane, this is my mother."

"Pleased to meet you, Mrs. Dalrymple."

"Hmmph."

Walt sensed this was not going well.

"I'm really sorry I threw you down like that, Mrs. Dalrymple, but you scared me, showing up out of nowhere and running at us like that."

"Hmmph."

Walt said, "Um, Mom, why are you here? Wait, no, uh, look, we're kind of in a hurry, and a lot of stuff is going on. C'mon, let's go upstairs."

"Now that makes sense. We need to get you into some dry clothes, young man." The middle-aged lady in the black polyester pantsuit grasped her son's elbow and strode toward the stairs, dragging him along as he looked back over his shoulder at Jane.

"I'm wet too," Jane muttered as she trailed behind.

They only stayed in the apartment long enough for Walt to grab his laundry bag and for Jane to towel off her face. Walt wrote a short note to Arlen and Marty saying that whatever had happened in the crashpad wasn't over and they should not open the door to anyone they didn't know. He left it on the spool table and hoped it would help.

Jane and Walt piled into Prince and headed for the Surf 'n Suds laundromat. Walt's mother followed in her Ford Falcon.

The Surf 'n Suds Washateria catered to college kids; thus it had a row of school desks instead of the usual plastic chairs. On a Wednesday night, it was home to only a few tired-looking kids studying to the sounds of washers and dryers and one hippie with his head down on a desk. When Jane went to the bathroom to change into the jeans and sweatshirt she'd borrowed at Walt's, his mother grabbed his elbow. "Who is this girl, Walt? How did you meet her?"

Well, gee, Mom, after the girl upstairs was shotgunned in the face, Jane came running to my place half-naked, and I hid her from a crazy guy who's probably a murderer, and tonight he kidnapped her, but I rescued her, and then we all fell in the water at the marina before we stole his car.

He was staring at his mother while this potential dialog ran through his head. She shook his arm. "Well?"

"Mom, she's a friend of mine—"

"I don't like girls like her."

"—and I met her a couple of days ago when there was some trouble at the apartment building."

"Probably one of those hippies. Walter, I want—"

No, Mom, the hippie chick is Needra, and she has a couple of joints in her purse.

For the first time in his life, Walter interrupted his mother. "Mom, we don't have a lot of time. Tell me why you're here."

Jane came back, carrying her dripping clothes and stuffing them into an empty washer. As he reached up to pull her hair back, it became abundantly clear that she had no bra under the t-shirt. Walt's mother pursed her lips and sniffed.

Jane said, "Look, why don't you go change, and we can put these in the washer." She looked at Mrs. Dalrymple. "We can answer all your questions, really."

Mrs. Dalrymple snapped, "Dry clothes can wait. I need to speak to my son." Walt had the feeling that if Jane said he needed oxygen, his mother would say that he could hold his breath. He peeled off his sweatshirt and the t-shirt under it, bent down, and unlaced his soggy Keds.

"I'll be right back." He really hoped they wouldn't be rolling around on the floor, scratching and pulling hair, when he returned. In the bathroom, he quickly pulled on dry pants and trotted back barefoot, carrying a dry t-shirt. The two women were watching the washing machine with lips pursed, squinty-eyed and silent.

Stuffing in his shirt, he said, "Mom, why are you here?" His mother looked significantly at Jane. "Tell me," he said. "Please."

Mrs. Dalrymple hesitated before reluctantly beginning to speak. "It's your father. Your father—he's acting very strangely, like always watching out the front window and always checking to make sure the doors are locked. I think it's something to do with your sister. He won't let her go out, and he wouldn't even let her go across the street to do homework with her little friend Linda."

"Penny? He won't let Penny go out? I don't understand." But Walt was afraid he did, at least part of it.

Ignoring him, Mrs. Dalrymple went on. "And I called and called, and there was no answer, so I drove up here. And I want to know what you are involved in, and I want to know right now."

"Mrs. Dalrymple, this can all be worked out and—"

"Excuse me, young lady, I am talking to my son."

"Mom, it's a long story." Something clicked. "Where's Dad? Right now, where is he?"

"Your father is out."

"Out where, Mom? Where is Dad?"

His mother rummaged in her purse for a tissue. "Your father is out buying a gun." Jane sucked in a breath and took Walt's arm. His mother grabbed the other arm and said, "I want you to come home. This is bad. You can tell me all about it on the way home." She tugged his arm. "I'm sure this girl will take care of your laundry, won't you, uh . . ."

"Jane, mom, her name is Jane."

"Yes, this girl will take care of your clothes." Walt's mom looked like she wanted to continue with how she was sure the girl knew all about boy's clothes, but she held back.

Walt said, "Tell me. Tell me now." He had never spoken to his mother like that in his life and her expression showed that she knew it. The amazing thing was that she didn't say anything about it. When she hesitated, he said, "Has somebody threatened Penny?"

"How did you – Never mind. Yes, I think someone is threatening your sister."

His mother tugged him toward the door, but Jane held on. Walt muttered, "Make a wish," and pulled both his arms free. "Mom, have you called the police?"

"Of course. They're watching the school. And there is a special officer assigned to the case. It's some sort of joint operation between two departments. But I want you home."

"I'll come as soon as I can, but right now, that's just not possible. I'm sorry, Mom, but Jane and I have some things we have to take care of."

His mother had her back turned, and she was walking toward the door. "When we get home, I'll make you beef stroganoff, and then we can have Coke floats for dessert." She saw he wasn't following, came back, and got his arm again. This time, when she pulled him toward the door, he was actually moving; the habit was that strong, a pull as powerful as her iron grip on his elbow and part of him said, *Go with her, go home and forget all this and everything will be like it was before and you won't have to figure out scary stuff.* He looked down at her hand, and it struck him. *She's old. She's old and scared, and she came up here to make sure I was okay when I didn't answer the phone. Her hand is wrinkled and spotted. She's old and scared, and it's somehow all connected to the shooting in the crashpad. It's my fault.* He found himself outside, opening the driver's door of the Falcon. He looked back and saw Jane standing in the doorway, backlit by the light from the laundry. His mother got in started the car.

He closed the door behind her. "Mom, I'm sorry, I'm not going with you."

"And we'll have pancakes for breakfast in the morning." His words registered. "Young man, you need to come home with me." She reached up to grasp at his arm, and her hand bumped the turn signal. It started flashing, the light reflecting off the other cars. Tick, tick. Go ahead, break your mother's heart. Tick, tick. Come on in.

"I can't go with you now." And he sensed that what he would say next would change everything, that he would never really go with her again, and his mother knew it too, that this last, desperate tightening of the apron strings was her last chance. He sighed. "I'm sorry. Tell Dad it will be all right. Please try to understand."

He expected an outburst, something along the lines of "Walter Dalrymple, get in the car this instant," but it didn't come. She seemed to wilt. "Walter, please. Your sister is upset. She's scared, and at the same time, she doesn't like being kept inside, and your father is frightening me, and now you are too. You, you are involved in this. Walter, it's not fair to do this to me. I'm not a young woman, and I can feel my heart racing. Please."

"If I stay here, I can fix it. I can make it all right. If I come home, it will be worse." His mother looked back at Jane standing in the doorway. "Mom," he said, "she's a nice girl. Really."

"Hmmph." Then she surprised him. She gripped the steering wheel, took a deep breath, and looked at him intently. "You look just like your father when he left for basic training. So young." Walt felt something shift between them, some elemental change that he didn't understand but that made him, what? Afraid? Oddly, no. "You can really fix this? Make these people not hurt Penny?"

"Yes."

She took a deep breath and squeezed his hand. "Then do it. What can I do to help?"

"Keep dad from going nuts with the gun."

She actually smiled a little. "I can do that, I think. This girl, what's-her-name, Walter, you're just a boy. You don't know about these things."

"I thought you said I looked like Dad."

"He was just a boy too."

The shift, whatever it was, was complete. *Tick tick. Come on in.* He said something in an attempt to make her feel a little better. "Mom, we haven't even been on a date."

She said, "If I think of something that will help, will you be home?"

"Uh, maybe. Leave a message with Arlen or Marty."

"All right. I'll call your father first. Now, give your mother a kiss." He did, and she drove away.

Back inside the laundromat, Jane was folding his clothes. She didn't look up.

He said, "They dried fast."

"Your mother doesn't like me."

"She's just upset about my sister. We need to talk. How well did you know Becky?"

"A couple of classes. We used to do homework together in the library."

"Did she have a job?"

"She worked in the circulation department at the library. Why?"

"Did she live at the crashpad?"

"Her roommate moved back home, so she was there while she looked for a new place. Why are you asking all these questions?"

"How did she know Morovich?"

"I don't know."

"How did you meet him?"

"It was a long time ago. Walt, you're making me nervous."

"We need to get out of here, hide out for a while."

"How about the lab? You keep promising."

"Two reasons not to. First, Morovich will know to look there, and second, I can't use the equipment until midnight."

"Morovich said we had forty-eight hours."

"You trust him?"

She nodded. "About that? Well, yeah, I think so. And I just thought of a place where nobody will find us. Okay, first things first. You've got dry clothes, but I need some of my own clothes."

"I can lend you some pants." He grinned, despite everything, "And there's always the sweatshirt."

She grinned right back. "I keep a change of clothes at the crashpad. If some girl hasn't borrowed them, I can change there."

"Don't you think—"

"We have time. He'll have to arrange transportation, and he won't look there, at least not for a while."

The crashpad actually looked a little better than the last time he'd seen it. The records were stacked next to the stereo, and thankfully, the turntable was no longer spinning. In his mind, he could hear the tick, tick. *Come on in! See the dead girl!* He could see through the short hall that the carpet in the bedroom was gone, leaving a bare wood floor. Jane stuck her head out of the second bedroom. "The dress is here. Five minutes." She vanished, and he heard the shower running. A couple of minutes later, she trotted out wearing a navy blue dress that stopped well above her knees carrying shoes and a large purse. "Here," she said, turning, "zip me up." For the rest of his life, Walt would remember the white bra strap and waistband of white panties. He decided life was good. All in all, this was worth getting thrown in the harbor.

And so Walt found himself, for the first time in his life, at a drive-in movie. And not just at a drive-in movie—he was at the Los Altos Drive-In off Bellflower Boulevard, so notorious that even he knew of it as a genuine passion pit, and he was with a girl.

Jane parked the Valiant in one of the back rows and then slid close on the bench seat. Seemingly of its own volition, his arm went around her, and when she turned her face up, he kissed her. And she kissed back. His other hand had ideas of its own too, and it slipped around her, pulling her close. Her breath quickened as he caressed her breast. He didn't even have time to be amazed; all he could think was: *It's going to happen It really is*, and Jane undid the buttons of his jeans.

She touched him and it was over.

Walter Dalrymple had never been so mortified in his entire life, and he'd had a lot of experience being mortified.

Jane whispered. "No problem, Walt. It'll be all right."

And by the time the second feature started, it was. He was, after all, barely eighteen.

The Girl in the Lab

At five minutes till midnight, Jane and Walt stood in the hall outside the basement laser lab in Science Building Number 1 with Walt holding his keys in his hand. He took a deep breath and looked at her, studying her carefully. Somehow, despite the drive-in, she looked perfect. She had restored her make-up, and her hair was back in its flip. He wanted to remember her like that, smiling, happy.

He said, "What happens when I open the door?"

"I don't understand."

"Do I get jumped? Beat up? What?"

"Walt, are you all right? You're not making sense." But she didn't sound puzzled. She sounded nervous.

"Well, you've wanted to visit the lab with me ever since we met. Now we're here. So, I'm curious about what happens next."

"Walt, what—"

"Oh, don't worry, I'll still open the door. I just like to know things." He looked at her intently.

She hesitated, edging away from him. "I haven't the slightest idea what you're talking about. And I'm hurt that you still don't trust me, even after—"

"All right, I'll tell you what I have figured out. First, you're a cop." Her eyes widened. "Second, Morovich is a cop too."

"Walt, don't be silly."

"Morovich is looking for this notebook."

She licked her lips. "Who have you told about this?"

Not how did you figure it out? Who have you told? "Nobody. Morovich wants the notebook. You want the notebook, but that's secondary. You are more interested in him. That makes you some kind of cop that investigates other cops, uh . . ."

She stood straighter. The nervousness vanished. "Internal affairs."

"And there's something about us being in the lab. Oh boy, now I'm catching on. It's something hidden in there that you think I can find. You've looked and couldn't find it. That's why you need me. Of course, it's about this notebook, but if it were the notebook itself, somebody would have found it, so it has to be something that will tell us how to find it, something you think I can figure out."

"How? How did you—"

"And if you get the notebook, you get Morovich. Figure it out? I should have caught on sooner, but I was distracted." He looked meaningfully at the swell of her breasts under the dress and felt a pang that he'd probably never get to touch them again. "First, it was you showing up at my door. You said Morovich made you take your clothes off, but you had your boots on. Not impossible, especially if you were pulling off a short skirt."

"I did. I mean, I was."

"But not quite right unless you really wanted to look sexy." She managed a weak grin. "And it worked. It was great." For a moment, his eyes unfocused and he stared over her shoulder. "Oh boy, I get it now. This all changed when Morovich shot Becky. You two are—were—partners. Anyway, the second point was how easy it all went. The cops questioned you briefly, probably just long enough for you to identify yourself. Then they cut you loose and kept me while you searched my apartment. But they didn't ask very many questions about Morovich, like what he was wearing, because they knew. Then Thibert and Minkoff showed up asking about a notebook."

"The search of your apartment was a bonus. It was—"

"Serendipity. Yeah. And when you helped me clean up, you knew where everything went. So now Morovich has gone off the reservation. Becky had something, a notebook, if I can believe anything anybody says, and he wants it. He'll kill to get it."

"Walt, I'm sorry. I never meant for it to get this out of hand. Truly. And I never lied to you, not exactly."

"True. For some reason, I neglected to ask if you were a cop. How long did it take you to set up the fake kidnapping?"

"I mean, it started small and then just got bigger and, wait, what about the kidnapping? When he stuffed me in the trunk?"

"Come on, I read private eye stories, and you knew it because I told you. The bad guy grabs you right in front of me? And the clue conveniently falls out of his pocket? Yeah, right. But the clincher was when I punched him. You misjudged me. You knew I was the playground punching bag, so you figured if I got to beat up a big guy I'd be ready to do anything you wanted. Except, when you're the school punching bag, you learn a lot about fights, and one thing I know for sure is even with a rock in my hand, I couldn't put him down that easy."

"You really did hurt him. I had to stall to make sure he didn't drown."

"Then, for some reason, you were willing to kill some time before coming here. That, I don't understand. I mean, it has to be something in here, I just don't know what."

"You haven't asked about the drive-in."

He said stiffly. "I prefer not to. So, I wonder. And that brings us full circle, doesn't it? Right back to my question."

She caught his arm, looked him in the eye. "The drive-in? That was real. I just wanted to be with you. Really. And it was nice." She smiled. "No, it was much better than nice. It was outta sight."

He believed her. He was, after all, barely eighteen.

"Yes, it was."

"I don't think your mother likes me."

"Well, since you're not going to tell me, let's open the door and see what happens." Unlocking the door saved him from responding to Jane's comment about his mother.

Inside, the laser lab looked normal. The laser itself was in the center of the room, a six-foot-long gray tube aimed at a target taped to a metal plate on the wall. Walt stopped and stood motionless in the center of the room. Along the left wall, there was a workbench lined with tall stools. As usual, there were half-full cups of machine coffee scattered around. A pile of white lab coats was draped over a lab stool. *The TA won't like that. They're supposed to be hung up in the closet.*

"See? It's just fine. No problem. This was a mistake, and we should go, okay? I've seen the lab, and it's very nice." From the doorway, Jane sounded nervous. As she watched Walt examine the lab, moving clockwise from left to right, she chewed her lower lip.

Walt didn't respond. He sniffed the air. "Smell that?"

"Sure. It's a laboratory, full of chemicals. C'mon, let's get my car and go back to my place."

"Biology is in SC-2. This is SC-1. We're smelling formaldehyde." And then Walt saw blood droplets on the floor.

"All right. Yeah, I need you to find the notebook. Becky said, 'PS I Love You,' over and over while Mo was hitting her, before he lost it and shot her, shot both of us, really. So, where is it?" He didn't answer. "Walt, is it here?"

Without turning from his careful examination of the lab, Walt said, "Unlikely. But if it is, will you turn him in? Or will the notebook vanish?"

"That is totally uncalled for, Walt. Uncalled for."

Sounds like my mother

"I think I'll leave you to walk back to your apartment," Jane said, but she made no move toward the door. "Why would the notebook vanish?"

"Because whatever's in it is bad for Morovich, probably incriminates him." He faced her. "What were you expecting to find here? Morovich, right? If I don't provide the notebook, you deliver me here." She couldn't meet his eyes. "But the plan has changed, hasn't it? He's not here."

"We need to leave."

He surprised himself. "Go ahead. I'm going to look around." *Lab coats. Not in the closet.*

Of course that was where he found her, the first place he looked, in the closet where people hung lab coats. She'd been stuffed in standing up, and when Walt opened the door, her pale, white arms stretched out, and her nude body tumbled into his arms, pushing him back a step in a cold waltz parody and he simply couldn't help it – the *Theme from a Summer Place* popped into his head and he thought of slow dancing with Jane. The dead girl's head was even resting on his shoulder.

Then he was backing up, hearing the "thump, thump," as her bare feet dragged over the lip of the closet. Despite missing a large portion of her skull and half her face, he knew it was Becky at once—the toe tag that flopped out, dangling from her right big toe as Walt caught her, was a giveaway. For a moment, his throat closed, and Walt felt the room shift in a slow, circular motion around him. He swallowed convulsively but was able to lower her to the floor. It seemed wrong to drop her. He cushioned what was left of her head and gently laid her down on her back. It seemed important not to drop her. *Tick, tick. Come on in. See the dead girl.* One blue eye—the only one she had left—stared at him.

"Oh my God." Jane squatted next to the corpse, looking at it closely.

"Got to be Morovich. He's been busy." Walt was surprised at how steady his voice was.

Jane looked up at him, frowning, pushing her bangs out of her face. Then she looked back at the dead girl. "She's been autopsied. They must have put a rush on it."

There was a y-shaped incision, two cuts starting at her shoulder blades, meeting in the center of her chest, where they joined into single cut that ran down past her navel. The cuts were now closed with large, careless stitches. Walt took somebody's lab coat off the pile on the stool and covered her, but it was too short, so her bare feet stuck out. Her toenails were painted red.

"Yeah. Oh boy. I really don't like this. Okay, Jane, you win. It's time to go." Walt was staring at the laser as if he'd never seen one before. Anything to avoid poor Becky. He felt an almost-uncontrollable urge to wash his hands. He got to his feet, unsteady but upright, and looked down at red toenails.

"Mister Upstanding Citizen, you mean you don't want to call the cops?"

"Anonymously, from a phone booth after we split."

Jane stood, brushing her hands against her dress, and said, "Walt, I am afraid that option is no longer available. Gone. All gone." She closed her eyes for a moment and then spoke without opening them. "Poor Becky. She was just a kid, you know? It was all a game to her. I tried to tell her."

"She stole the notebook."

"Worse. She stole it, and she figured out what it meant, and the little fool even told me. God, she was dumb! But she was only nineteen. You're allowed to be when you're that young."

He almost blurted out, *I'm only eighteen.* Barely. Instead, he forced himself to take a deep breath and turn to look Jane in the eye. "Jane, what does Morovich think? If you get the book, will you turn him in?"

"Yes. At this point, he has to assume that I will."

"You better tell me what's in the notebook."

"No! No way, Walt! Then he'll be after you too."

"Jane, he's going to be after me anyway. He has to assume I know, just like you turning him in. He can't take the chance. So, either way, I'm a dead man, so tell me right now." She shook her head. He sighed. "All right. We need to call the cops. I'm not an expert, but somehow I think stealing a body from the morgue is against the law."

"It is. But Walt, I've changed my mind. Somebody else needs to report it. Becky's dead. We can't help her. Come on."

She grabbed his elbow. He wished people would quit doing that. He said, "Why did he put her here? Obviously, for us to find. He's sending a message." Despite himself, he started to think, to process the information he had in order to figure it out.

From the first moment Walt had looked into Morovich's eyes, he had understood that he was one of the bullies who were truly dangerous, the kind he'd met only twice before. So it was time to stop thinking about Jane, warm and soft and curvy under the blue dress. If Morovich killed him, he'd never get a chance to be with her again. "And the message is what? That he can get into the morgue? That he wants us to know he's serious? We knew that. He wants to muddy the water, but doing this will keep me from finding the notebook." He looked around the lab again, avoiding poor Becky. The lab coat wasn't so bad, but her feet . . . "Jane, what happens if *nobody* finds this notebook?"

"If it's what we think, several murders go unsolved. Why?"

"Maybe he's decided that if he can't find it and I can't find it, nobody can. So what does he think we'll do when we find Becky here in the lab? He knows we won't call the cops; that would mean hours of questioning while he's loose. Uh-oh."

Jane was going through the room, opening drawers, looking in cabinets .She said, "What are you thinking? Please tell me it's something good. Maybe we need to run."

"Not just yet." Walt looked at the blood drops on the floor. *Dead people don't bleed, not after they've been dead overnight.* The drops weren't circular; they had little points on one side, and the points led to the door connecting the laser room with the small classroom next door. The door, usually locked, was open. Inside, they found Stanley Thibert, still in the same bad blue suit, sitting in one of the desks, his chin propped on his hand, in the same position that generations of students have assumed as they've fallen asleep in class—except that Thibert had a bullet hole in the center of his forehead.

Walt said, "We were both wrong. Morovich wasn't around the bend when he killed Becky. *Now* he's around the bend."

"Small-caliber, probably a .22. No exit wound. Minimal blood. Marks around the wound indicate close range."

"Thanks, Jane, I really needed to know that. Time for you to tell me about this guy and his partner." Walt stepped back from the body, but bumped the back of the chair.

Thibert's chin slid off his hand and he slowly bent forward until his forehead rested on the desk.

Jane said, "Rigor hasn't set in yet. Okay, I don't know much about these guys. They used to be cops. Now they're freelance."

"Why do they want the notebook?"

"I don't know for sure."

"Jane."

"I think they paid Becky for information. She was sleeping with Morovich, and he confiscated drugs from people he busted and shared the drugs with her. She stole the notebook from him, probably because she wanted to have something to hold over him, maybe just because she felt like it. Anyway, Thibert and Minkoff found out, and they wanted it. Morovich wanted to beat them to it."

"I've never understood that. Becky's got the notebook, but why kill her?"

"She hid it. I think she was spaced out. You know she did a lot of acid? She was kind of messed up. Anyway, all she would say was 'PS I Love You.' And she tried to give him a library book."

"What?"

"She gave Morovich a book, or tried to. It was useless."

"'PS I Love You.' The Beatles song. My little sister Penny plays their albums constantly."

"She just kept saying it over and over. Then he shot her. And he would have killed me."

"Oh, yeah. I read that in *Playboy's* article on 'How to Pick up Chicks.' Shoot and kill her friend, and she'll follow you anywhere. So, why were you working with him?"

"He wasn't always crazy. It's not always easy for a woman on the force, but he sort of took me under his wing."

"Go on."

"I thought I loved him. I really did. I did well in the academy, and I got this assignment for, uh, personal reasons."

"Okay, now, one more time, for the sixty-four-thousand-dollar question: what's in the notebook?"

"Can you find it?"

"Yes. What's in it?"

"Walt, it's better if I don't tell you."

"We've been over this. Someone is threatening my family, and Morovich is not the best candidate, he's the only one. Occam's razor."

"What?"

"The simplest explanation is usually correct. When you hear hoof beats, you think horses, not zebras."

She looked at him strangely and shook her head. "It's a list of names. Cops."

"Crooked cops? Stealing from druggies? I've heard about that."

She shook her head. "Worse. Much worse."

"Jane, just tell me."

She took a deep breath. "It was murder for hire and, and sometimes girls." Seeing his look, she went on hurriedly, as if telling it quickly made it easier. "Girls, young, cute. Hippie chicks. Sometimes they'd just, you know, vanish. I think, no, I'm pretty sure they were sold." She saw the look on his face. "But Mo never had anything to do with that part of it. I called him 'Mo,'" she finished lamely. "Look, I know you're really smart, but you have to believe me. He will hurt you, and me too. He has nothing to lose. I guess they don't either."

"Minkoff and Thibert? Well, we don't have to worry about Thibert anymore."

"Yeah. I assume they're in it."

Walt stared off into space a moment. "There are three options. One, we find the book and give it to the police. Two, we find the book and give it to Morovich. Three, we find the book and keep it. It's insurance."

She nodded. "We have to turn it in. They'll all be locked up."

Walt frowned. "Including Morovich. I can't believe internal affairs would send his ex-, uh, girlfriend to spy on him."

"Who better? That's why I got the job."

"You mean he didn't suspect you?"

"Of course he did. No, he knew I was IA. He just thought, you know, that I still loved him and he could turn me, that I'd never really rat him out."

Walt muttered, "In *Dune*, Frank Herbert says, 'Better the knife you see than the one you don't.' I'm paraphrasing."

"Who? Herb?"

"Never mind. And he was almost right, wasn't he?"

She blushed and nodded. "You may not believe this, but it came down to the oath I took. I have to turn him in."

"Option One. Good."

"You were testing me!"

Walt took another quick look around the classroom. When he found nothing, he said, "Right. Time to go."

"If we get the notebook, we'll be able to identify some cops we can trust, because they won't be in it. Before that . . ."

"Okay, we just have to find the notebook. To do that, we have to hide out till morning, which shouldn't be too hard; it's a big campus."

"You know, we could take a chance. I mean, what are the odds we'd hit a crooked cop? We could probably go to the police."

Walt shook his head. "I don't think it's really random. Morovich will figure that we might do that and plant one of his buddies where he could intercept us. Once that happens, he can get the information out of us one way or another."

"Oh."

"It's what I would do."

"What happened to the nice, innocent guy who saved my ass?"

"He's here, and he's glad he saved it. It's a fine ass." Walt was amazed at his boldness. Later, he put it down to temporary hysteria caused by finding not one, but two dead bodies in one day, but it was the first time he had ever said the word "ass" to a girl. He turned bright pink. Jane laughed.

She took his arm. "Okay, Mr. Smarty, what now? Run?"

"Yes. It could be worse. All we have to do is hide."

Outside in the hall, Walt locked the door behind him, and they hurried up the stairs to the ground floor. Jane grabbed his collar, hauled him back before he could open the door, and said, "Okay, we need to go slow here. Keep your eyes peeled."

"I never understood that expression. Makes no sense." But he only opened the door a crack.

When they peeked out of the stairwell and looked down the hall, they saw his roommate Arlen and Walt's mother on the outside of the glass doors, shading their eyes and peering in. Walt threw the stairwell door open and stepped out. When Arlen spotted them, he looked relieved and mouthed, "Let us in," as he pointed down at the crash bars on the inside. Walt's mother had crossed her arms under her breasts. Walt and Jane stopped and stared. For a moment, Walt thought he was imagining it; they couldn't really be there. He blinked, and they were still there, only now they were both impatient, Arlen making more urgent arm motions at the crash bars and Walt's mother tapping her foot.

"She's tapping her foot," Walt muttered.

"Bad?"

"There was an incident with a small rocket . . ."

"A rocket?"

"It was small, a one-stage."

"And your mother tapped her foot?"

It was clear neither of them wanted to open the door.

"I'm considering locking myself in with the dead bodies."

"Bad idea, Walt. Don't be silly. This is serious."

"Yeah. She'd just get somebody to open the door."

His paralysis forgotten, Walt rushed down the hall and pushed the doors open. He pulled both of them in and closed the door behind them before asking the obvious question. "What are you two doing here? Mom, I thought you went home."

His mother turned on Jane, her hands on her hips. "What have you gotten my son into?" She stared at Jane and then at Walt as he stood next to the blonde in the short blue dress. Her lips pursed. She stepped forward and put herself between Jane and her son. "Walter, we will talk later."

Jane opened her mouth, but before she could speak, Walt took his mother by the shoulders. "Mom, please. What did you find out when you called home?"

"How did you know I called home?"

"Mom, we don't have much time. Okay, okay. You went back to the apartment to call home and tell Dad you had talked to me. Something he said made you decide to stay here and find me. Arlen was in the apartment and said he knew where I'd be later. Okay?"

"When you say it like that it sounds simple." She reached up and touched his cheek. "My boy. My smart, smart boy."

"Mom, just tell me."

"You remember I was worried about your father?"

"Yes."

"Well, when I talked to him, I got him to tell me why he was even more upset. We got a note and one of those Polaroid pictures of your sister on the playground."

"Tell me what the note said."

"You have forty-eight hours. I mean, it was addressed to you, but your father opened it, and it said, 'You have forty-eight hours.'"

Walt could feel Jane standing next to him. He would not look at her. Forty-eight hours. "Actually less, because Dad held the note for a while. What else?"

"Well, they want you to find something." *Yep, that's it.* He closed his eyes for a moment.

"After the note arrived," his mother continued, "the phone rang, and a man said for you to find it. Your father, Walter, I've never seen him like this, never. He scares me. I don't know what he'll do, and I don't think he does either."

Jane said softly, "Forty-eight hours."

Walt said grimly. "A notebook, right?" His mother nodded. "Mom, what did the cop look like? The one who said it was a joint operation."

Jane sucked her breath in and murmured, "Oh boy." She clutched his elbow.

"The cop at the school? I never saw him, did I? But the teacher said he looked like a fireplug."

Now Walt looked at Jane. "There was time yesterday. He could have driven down to Oceanside and back."

Jane pushed her bangs up, out of her face. "But how did he know?"

He didn't answer her. Instead, he turned to his roommate. "Arlen, after they found the body upstairs, they questioned you, right?"

"You found the body. It was you. Yeah, the cops talked to me a little, along with everybody in the building."

"They asked you about your roommates." It was not a question.

Arlen could only nod, his hair falling over his face. He kept looking toward the doors.

"All right. Mom, here's what I need you to do. Call Dad. Tell him that if the people contact him again, he should tell them I can find what they're looking for. I know where it is. And if anything, anything at all, happens to my sister they will never see it, but the wrong people will. I promise that." Jane was staring at him. He turned to his roommate.

"Arlen, I need you to drive my mother back to get her car. She can call from a pay phone. Then, Mom, you go home, and Arlen, you bail, find a . . . Oh, hell. Marty. Get Marty, and both of you get out. Find an all-night movie or something."

Mrs. Dalrymple said, "I see a pay phone right down the hall."

"Marty's off at some football thing tonight, meet the cheerleaders or something. Must be nice."

"No, Mom, you need to go."

"Nonsense, I'll call your father from here. It will be quicker."

"Bad idea, Mom." She started to ask why when they heard sirens in the distance. "That's why," Walt said. "We have to run. Now."

"I've done nothing wrong. Walter, why do we need to run?" She was talking to her son but glaring at Jane.

Jane said, "Mrs. Dalrymple, there are two dead bodies back there in the lab."

Walt sighed. "Actually, one of them is in the classroom next to the lab."

Jane finished, "And if you are found with them, your only phone call will be to an attorney."

Arlen had trotted to the doors, and he peered out. "Lights turning into the parking lot next to the construction. Nope, they're jumping the curb and coming across the quad. Bitchin.'"

His mother decided. "All right." She started for the doors.

"Not that way. Come on. There's a way to get to SC-2." Walt switched off the hall lights, cutting the illumination to the nighttime energy-saving one tube per fixture. All at once, it was easier to see outside. More lights turned into the upper parking lot. Walt hustled them to the stairs to the basement. Mrs. Dalrymple stumbled halfway down, but Jane caught her, steadied her, and got the older woman's hand on the railing.

At the bottom, Walt led the way down the hall, away from the lab. In addition to the laser lab, this lower level was used for storage. It was also lit by fluorescent tubes in ceiling fixtures, but several of them were out, creating pools of darkness while others buzzed and flickered. "Oh, this is nice," Arlen muttered.

Walt said, "They don't bother with the ballasts down here, so the lights go out." Nobody bothered asking him to explain his newest bit of trivia. Being used to this lack of response when he presented interesting facts, he went on anyway. "Ballasts regulate the current to fluorescent lights; without a ballast, the light would draw too much." Jane patted his arm as they hurried down the hall toward the east end, away from the quad and police.

The passage had a gouged tile floor; it was walled in beige cinderblock, wide enough for them to walk side by side except where equipment was parked against the wall. Space was at a premium in the science building—the hall was lined with equipment on wheeled carts, some shrouded, some uncovered and dusty. Halfway down, they came to a gray metal door on the left side. "This leads to SC-2, the next building to the north. It was put in to move equipment, but it's not used much anymore." He stood in front of it, methodically going through the keys on his key ring.

"How did you find it?"

"Mom, I'm kind of busy here." He reached the last key and froze. None of them looked right. "I, um, there's lots of free time when you're running experiments. I sort of explored."

Jane was more to the point. "Key?" The tube overhead buzzed, flickered, went out, and then blinked back on before it buzzed one more time, feebly, and gave up. Sudden darkness pooled around the door.

Walt muttered, "Ballast," again. No one asked for more explanation. Down the hall, another tube didn't bother flickering; it just went off with a pop that made them all jump.

He started going through the keys again, this time by touch, feeling the notches, measuring the length against the first joint of his thumb, one at a time. At last he said, "Got it." He felt for the keyhole, found it, inserted the key, and turned the lock, and the door opened. He groped for the switch, found it, flicked the lights on, and held the door while the other three went in. "Stay quiet. They'll be on the ground level by now." He gently pulled the door closed and started toward the other end with the others trailing along behind.

At the end, they found stairs leading up to a set of double doors. Walt said, "This building doesn't have a basement, so we have to be careful"—Arlen sprinted to the doors and pushed one open—"because they could see us. Geez, Arlen, take it easy."

His roommate whispered, "I can do this," stuck his head out for a moment and pulled it back. Then he bent low and darted out into the hall, where he peered out the double doors. A moment later, he hurried back. "Okay, I see lights flashing; we got fuzz outside SC-1. Three cars, looks like one campus rent-a-cop and two Long Beach. Lot of guys standing around." Lights flared briefly, moving across the wall opposite them. "Uh-oh, must be more fuzz coming."

"Young man, I was brought up to respect law enforcement officers. They are not fuzz or pigs; they are defenders of society." Everyone stared at Mrs. Dalrymple as she finished this speech. She straightened her jacket and sniffed. "Well, they are, aren't they? I still think we should simply go out there and explain what happened. I am certain my son and Arlen have nothing to fear." She looked at Jane significantly.

"Mom, we have less than forty-eight hours. Remember the note and the phone call."

"I haven't forgotten. The police will help us, and they will protect your sister."

Jane muttered, "The right ones will. The wrong ones will blow our heads off."

Mrs. Dalrymple rounded on her. "Young woman, I will thank you to keep out of a family discussion that has nothing to do with you."

"Mom, that's not fair. Jane—"

Arlen interrupted. "Am I the only one who remembers the cops are coming? We need to run or turn ourselves in, but just standing here waiting is a bad idea. And Walt's the one with the Berkeley scholarship to protect."

"This way."

"No! Walter, this time I have to put my foot down. Do we have any other options? I think not. We are going to the police."

Jane said, "Mrs. Dalrymple, I *am* a police officer."

Arlen snorted. "Yeah, and I'm Spiro Agnew."

Now Walt's mother turned on him. "And just what does that mean? Young man, do you think women can't be police officers?"

"Girls? Well, no, they're not suited for it."

"And why not?" Walter had seen her lips pursed like this before, but not very often.

Arlen turned to Walt. "Your mother's a libber?"

Walt was speechless. His mother said grimly, "I do not speak of it often, but I was a welder at Consolidated Aircraft in San Diego while Walter's father, Tom, was in Europe. When the war ended, of course we were all glad and most of us just wanted to go home, but some girls wanted to keep their jobs, and did that happen? No! The men took them away." To Jane, she said, "Young lady, are you a police officer?" Jane could only nod before this bulldozer of a woman. "And you say we should not go to the police?"

"If we do they will hold us for questioning, and Walt won't be able to find what he needs to in order to keep your daughter safe. I'm sorry."

All Walt could say was, "You were a welder?"

The old lady made sense. Jane was not as surprised as she might have been. She had met a woman Mrs. Dalrymple's age on the force who'd had the same grim look and pursed lips like that on the day she'd been forced into retirement.

Jane turned to Walt. "Look, it's time for you to tell me where it is. We may have to split up."

Arlen chimed in. "Yeah, we deserve to know."

Walt's mother laughed. "Walter, let me tell them. My son doesn't know where this mysterious notebook is." They all stared. "He's my son, isn't he? I remember when he built a water and compressed-air rocket, and I asked him if it was safe to shoot off in the back yard, and he said he was sure it was."

"Mom, this is beside the point."

"He has that same look now."

Walt looked at Jane, "I paid for the window out of my allowance."

She said, "Walt, I really don't care."

Arlen muttered, "Quiz kid," and trotted to the doors and peeked out again. When he came back, he said, "Whatever we do, it better be quick. Somebody just drove up on one of those little carts, and they're unlocking the doors to SC-1. It won't be long till they find the bodies."

Mrs. Dalrymple looked at her son fondly. "But you can find it, can't you? This notebook." He nodded. She turned to Walter's roommate. "Arlen, you and I are going out that door and meeting the police. We will tell them the truth, won't we? I came here to talk to my son, but we couldn't get into the lab. Walter and this young woman will find whatever it is."

Walter was shaking his head. "It won't work, Mom. The, the notebook is about crooked cops, and if you run into one of them, they'll use you to make me do what they want. Or they may hurt you. No, we stick together. And we run."

"Crooked cops?"

"That's what everybody's looking for. A list of names, bad cops."

"Oh my. Son, I have to tell you. I believe your father will shoot anyone he thinks will harm your sister. Anyone."

Walt closed his eyes for a moment. Then he said, "Good. This way." He led them to the stairs. "Stay close."

On the second floor he unlocked one of the labs. The furniture had been removed and the walls were stripped down to the metal studs. "They're remodeling this lab. I saw this the other day." One of the windows had its glass removed, and they saw a large, dirty canvas tube leading down into darkness. "This goes down into a big dumpster on the ground level. It's on the other side of the building, so they won't see us."

Arlen said, "No way, Jose. Who knows what we'll land on? This thing is for construction debris like busted-out walls and shit." He looked abashed. "Er, sorry, Mrs. Dalrymple. Pardon my French."

Jane said, "Let's just go out the back door before anybody gets there." She grinned at Walt. "Occam's razor, right?"

Mrs. Dalrymple was quiet.

Walt said, "No, we need to be where this comes out. If we go out the back door, we'll get caught."

"What about the stuff in the dumpster? The stuff that will poke large holes in us?" Arlen chimed in.

Walt said, "Yeah. I'm thinking, I'm thinking. Okay, look, I'll go first. The trick will be pressing your arms and legs against the canvas as you descend. The friction will slow you down." *I hope*, he thought. "I'll go first to make sure it works, and I'll be at the bottom, waiting to help."

His mother came over and kissed him on the cheek. She looked at the tube and then faced them. "If my son says it will work, then it will work. But Walter, I can't go with you, can I? You must know that. I will simply wait here. Who knows, perhaps I won't even be found until class starts, and I can pretend to be a visiting professor."

"Mom, you can do it."

"When I was a girl—her age—I wouldn't hesitate. I was on my high school girls' basketball team, you know." Actually, he didn't know that about her. People were full of surprises.

Jane walked over and studied the canvas tube.

"Wait." Walt ran out into the hall, and they heard breaking glass. A minute later, he ran back in holding the nozzle end of a fire hose, dragging the length behind him. "We can tie this around your waist and lower you down."

Arlen said, "Oh, man, I don't know."

Jane said, "Walt, it may not reach the bottom."

His mother looked at him. Then she simply took the hose and began tying it around her waist.

Arlen muttered, "Holy shit. We're really gonna do this. Sorry, ma'am."

Mrs. Dalrymple, the basketball-playing welder, mother of three, was shifting her purse around to her back. "Hell yes, kid. Let's go." She had a wild look in her eyes, and the look and the toothy grin, combined with his father buying a gun, made Walt began to wonder if both his parents weren't crazy. It would explain a lot.

Walt said, "Okay. I'm first. Then Jane. Arlen, you lower Mom down as far as you can and then climb down. That way, Jane and I will be there to catch her and you can help her get started. And Jane, Jane?"

He turned to see blonde hair disappearing down the chute. His mother was standing next to the mouth, holding Jane's hand with a, wrist-to-wrist, trapeze-artist grip. His mother's feet were spread wide, and she had one hand braced against the windowsill. Jane's voice came from the chute, slightly muffled. "Okay, it's not that far down from here, and the slope isn't as bad as I thought it would be. Just be sure to push against the canvas as hard as you can." Walt's mother staggered back as Jane let go of her hand, and almost sat down hard. There was a crash and then silence. Suddenly the filthy contents of the tube were lit from within.

Walt ran to the gaping mouth and stuck his head in. "Jane? Jane!"

She looked up at him from only a few feet down and took a small silver flashlight out of her mouth. "You don't have to yell. I'm right here. And we have a problem. The workers have clogged the chute with stuff, feels like broken drywall. I'm maybe two-thirds of the way down." There was the sound of breaking drywall. "I'm trying to squash it down more." There was more crunching. "Oh, barf."

"What?"

"Walt, this really groovy escape route was also used by the workers for their garbage. I'm standing on what looks like half a sandwich and, oh, that's so nice, and I just put my hand on something squishy that I *really* hope is a piece of rotted fruit."

His mother handed Walt the hose. "Hold this." And before he could stop her, she put one hand on his shoulder and hoisted herself up to sit on the lip of the chute, put both hands on the top of the metal ring, and was lowering herself down. With no other options, he looped the hose around his waist and tried to control his mother's descent. She twisted around and looked up at the last moment, and then she vanished into the dark, grinning and wild, saying, "Bombs away!" as she dropped while clutching the fire hose.

Arlen grabbed the hose and took some weight. "She's batshit, man. Batshit."

Reluctantly, Walt said, "No, I get it. She's small enough to fit next to Jane, and she's got the line, so maybe if we have to, we can get them back up."

"Looniness runs in your family, doesn't it?"

Walt didn't respond—this was too close to his own thinking.

There was more crunching, and then Jane said, "I think we're going to make it. I see light." A moment later, they heard, "Okay, Mrs. Dalrymple, let me slide down first."

"Edna."

"What?"

"Call me Edna. And I still don't like you."

"Back at you, Edna. Okay, here goes." A moment later, Jane called up, "Okay, I'm standing on top of stuff in the dumpster. Edna Dalrymple, come on down." Walt and Arlen played out more fire hose.

After a moment of muttered exclamations and scraping, sliding sounds, Edna called up, "Made it! Walter, I am untying the fire hose from my waist, so you boys use it to climb down. Be careful to go slow and watch where you put your feet."

"Yes, Mom."

He couldn't believe he'd said that. He felt like he was about nine years old.

Arlen said, "Might be a good idea to hurry. I think I hear voices."

He held the hose while Arlen stuck his feet in and scooted over the edge. After his roommate was down, Walt looked for something to tie the hose to so he could use it to lower himself, but he could find nothing; the room had been stripped for remodeling. He dragged out as much hose as he could, but he was worried about time. It seemed right to fold the hose and put it back in the wall case, but he decided the cops would see the broken glass and figure it out, and anyway, that was nuts, and last, but far from least, this was taking longer than he had planned. He gave up and went into the tube feet first. Pressing arms and legs against the side, he slowed his fall a little, but it was still dark, dirty, and scary as his Keds bumped across metal ribs that held the chute open and dust was forced up his nose and into his eyes, and once, his hand rubbed across something cold and gooshy sticking to the canvas that he really hoped was Jane's rotted fruit. Reflexively he jerked his hand away, and whatever it was slapped into his forehead, rolled down across his mouth, and slid off his neck. *That wasn't fur, was it?* But in seconds, he was landing on crumpled drywall scraps. Hands grabbed his feet and pulled him out of the opening into the overflowing dumpster, where the others were standing on piles of trash, waiting for him.

Arlen looked over the edge and then climbed out. Jane put one hand on the rim, vaulted over, and said, "Okay, Edna, this'll be easy—you just sit on the lip, swing your legs over, slide off, and we'll catch you."

The older woman didn't hesitate; she just sat, turned, and dropped. She landed and stumbled, but Jane and Arlen were there to catch her. Walt carefully climbed out, dropped to the asphalt, and for a moment, they just stood and gaped at each other in the moonlight. They were covered in white drywall dust, with occasional spots of nasty unidentifiable stuff. His mother reached out and flicked something off his shoulder. Suddenly they were pointing and laughing, and Walt thought it might be all right after all.

Jane said, "Okay, Walt, here we are, only a little the worse for wear. Now what?"

"We need wheels. They park the carts on the other side of that hedge." His mother looked confused, so he added, "The campus uses these oversize golf carts to haul stuff around. There should be a few over there."

"Won't they be locked?"

"I'm counting on Jane to hotwire one. Let's go."

What they found on the other side of the hedge was better than a golf cart; it was not one, but two golf-cart-sized pickups, with no cabs over the bench seats and canvas shells over the truck beds. Walt said, "Jane, do your thing." She pursed her lips, looked at the dash, and then shrugged and crawled under it. She was tugging on wires when Arlen ran from the other truck waving keys.

"I found 'em! I found some keys! Found 'em under the seat of that other little truck." He stopped, panting. "I found the keys."

Jane reached up, grabbed the steering wheel, and used it to haul herself out from under the dash. "That's a good thing, since I don't think I could get this one started."

Walt took the keys. "Pile in, everybody. Mom, you and Arlen better get in the back." He started to get behind the wheel, and then he looked at Jane and muttered, "Yeah, yeah. Go ahead. The cops will be here in a minute or two." She grinned and slipped behind the wheel.

"Kid, we're already here." Morovich stepped out of the shadows. He was holding a shotgun. "I think we should all go for a ride. There's an item that belongs to me that you need to get."

Jane said, "Mo, please, don't make this worse."

"Oh, yeah, like I'm going to listen to the bitch that sold me out."

Walt said, "What happened to forty-eight hours?"

"Gee, I must have had my fingers crossed."

"Hurt my sister, and I won't get the notebook for you." Walt sounded like he meant it.

"Kid, this is a real unhealthy time for you to grow a pair."

Walt started to say, "Huh?" but his mother cut him off. "Young man, my husband is waiting for you, and he has a gun. He was a soldier, wasn't he? He was one of the men who waded ashore on D-Day. That's right, one of those heroes, so if you have any thought that he might not use it, you can just forget that this instant. This instant!" She dusted off the sleeve of her pantsuit jacket and glared at him defiantly, a middle-aged lady facing down a gun-toting psychopath. Walt decided insanity did run in his family, but he was so proud of her he wanted to cheer. Then she spoiled the impression by sitting on the truck's tailgate and rubbing her ankle.

"Mom, here, scoot in next to Arlen." She moved in. Between the two of them, she and Arlen filled the tiny truck bed. Walt shut the tailgate and turned to Morovich. He wasn't sure what he was going to say, but as it turned out, it didn't matter.

"Man, you are so easy to follow. You never did undercover work like we did." Leonard Minkoff stepped out of the shadows behind Morovich and pointed a large revolver at him, or maybe he pointed it at the little truck with Walt and company in it. Mostly he just waved it around. "Where's Stan? He was supposed to meet me."

Walt didn't want to be around for the answer to that. "Look," he said, "you guys don't need to do it this way. I'm going to get the notebook, really. I just can't get it for a while."

He touched Jane's leg. She nodded slightly. He stepped away from the truck, walked over to the passenger side, and stood there. "I can tell you— Now! Duck!" Jane pushed the accelerator to the floor as Walt dove in, landing in the footwell. The little truck wasn't all that fast, but Morovich and Thibert were ten yards away and taken by surprise. The truck bounced over the curb and headed up East Campus Drive. For a minute or two the two men with guns actually ran after them.

"He didn't shoot!" Arlen shouted from the back. He sounded amazed.

"Most people's reaction time is 1.7 seconds from the time they see something. And he couldn't risk it with the other cops so close. They'd hear it, and anyway, they need us alive." Walt, trying to climb out of the footwell, sounded relieved too. He finally got turned around and slid up onto the passenger seat.

"You mean he needs *you* alive," Arlen muttered. "We may not be as important to him."

Walt didn't have anything to say to that, since it was obviously true. Instead, he said, "Pull in here." He pointed and Jane turned the truck into a faculty parking lot half-full of stacks of lumber slated for one of the ongoing campus construction projects. "Okay, help me take the top off this thing." Arlen and Jane hopped out and started unfastening the snaps that held the canvas top on.

Arlen said, "Walt, why are we doing this? There's two crazy Ho-Dads with guns after us." He paused, holding the edge of the canvas. "We need to, you know, hide until we can get the notebook."

"He's not really after us. He wants the notebook. I find it and hand it over to him, and we're cool. Right now he'll settle for following us, and then take the notebook away once we find it for him."

"All right, so why jump out of the shadows and point a shotgun at us?"

"He wants us scared. If Jane hadn't driven off he would have let us go, I think." All at once, Walt stopped and stood perfectly still, staring off into the darkness. "Mom, what did you say Morovich sent to the house?"

"A picture of your sister's schoolyard. Why?"

"What kind of picture?"

"One of those instant ones, a—"

"Polaroid."

"Yes, son. Why?"

"I need to think for a minute." He walked off into the darkness, vanishing behind a pile of two-by-fours.

Arlen said, "What the hell? I am not stoked about hanging out here, you know? Not stoked at all."

Jane and Edna said together, "Just finish taking the top off." Then they glared at each other.

Jane said, "Put it in the back. Spread it out over the truck bed."

Walt came back, looking grim. "Jane, what's in this notebook?"

"I told you, a list. It might implicate cops in crimes, including murders."

"I think it's more. I think there are pictures pasted in it." She stared at him. "Proof."

She closed her eyes. "Proof of death." The others looked confused, so she went on. "Contract killers often take a picture or a, a"—she swallowed—"a trophy to prove to their customer that they killed who they were paid to." Nobody asked what she meant by "a trophy." "I always wondered why Morovich was so worried about notes. You know, anybody could scribble stuff about cops. But if it contains proof, he's screwed. Polaroids of dead bodies would do it, especially since he's already under suspicion."

Walt said, "And so are we, screwed, I mean. If I find the notebook, he knows I'll look in it. Then he has to kill me."

Jane looked at him. "And if you don't find it, he kills you anyway. And maybe your sister as a bonus." She looked down at her feet. "Walt, I'm so sorry I got you into this."

"I always wondered why you chose our apartment."

"Becky told me about the guys in the apartment downstairs. About you. She said to tell you the song."

"PS I Love You."

"She said you'd help. You'd know what she meant."

Walt thought Jane meant that he'd be a sucker for a bare-breasted chick, but that's not the sort of thing you say in front of your mother. "I was having a good time until the part about my sister and my dad with a gun."

"Well, I'm not having a good time." Arlen sounded scared.

"Yeah, about that. Listen, Arlen, Morovich doesn't know you. Neither does Thibert. You're clear now. I need you to do something. Take my mother and hide somewhere. Mom, get to a phone and call Dad and tell him not to do anything crazy. This will all be over by morning."

Arlen didn't hesitate, just clapped Walt on the back and said. "Bitchin'. Good luck, man. I'd stay if I thought there was anything I could do. You know I would."

"No, son, I want to stay." His mother sounded like she meant it.

"How's your ankle, Mom?"

"What? My ankle? Why, I'm fine. Right as rain."

"The right answer was 'Why do you ask?' You turned it jumping out of the dumpster."

"Oh. You saw."

"You're my mom. Of course I saw."

"Well, I still want to stay. Walt, I can't walk all the way to your apartment."

"She stays, I stay."

"Arlen, no."

"You think I want to be running around the campus at midnight with the cops and not one, but two, count 'em, two psycho killers looking for me?"

"Minkoff might not be psycho. He might just be a killer," Walt muttered. Suddenly he said, "Jane, where do *you* think the notebook is?"

"Me? Why? I mean, I really don't have any idea. I just hoped you did."

"I need to get into Morovich's head. He may figure this out, and we don't need him to get there first. In fact . . . I wonder if Minkoff and Morovich have joined forces, or are they competing for the notebook? They didn't seem all that friendly."

Jane said, "Minkoff must be in the notebook."

"Yeah." He thought for a moment. "We need to hide."

Arlen said, "Bitchin'. First sensible thing you've said."

Jane elbowed him. "C'mon, you loved sliding down the trash chute."

"I will love getting my fake ID and going to the 49'er Tavern and drinking as many giant honking schooners of beer as I can before I fall off the bar stool, and then I want one poured down my throat. So, now what?"

Reluctantly Walt said, "Yeah, well, I do sort of need you. Everybody get back in the truck and crawl under the canvas. Jane, you drive."

"I found the keys, so I should get to drive. Where are we going?"

"Okay, Arlen, okay. The library. The notebook is in the library. Go up East Campus Drive, turn right, and we can park in the staff lot behind the library. We're in a campus truck."

Jane cupped his chin in her palm and looked at him intently. "Walt, honey, *where* in the library? You need to narrow it down."

He grinned. His mother smiled complacently and said, "PS I Love You."

At last, Jane shrugged. She shook Walt's chin back and forth. "This better work."

"You'll see."

So, Arlen drove the truck, minus the top, back up East Campus Drive, toward the library. Walt was right—the police activity at SC-1 had convinced Thibert and Morovich to take cover. But as the truck crested the hill, they saw lights and moving figures at the intersection, blocking their way to the library parking lot.

"Good thing I left the lights off," Arlen said as he turned the truck around.

Walt said, "Go back down the hill and turn left. We'll go up the west side of the campus. We can get into the library parking lot that way."

After only two left turns, they found cars, many with fraternity or sorority decals, filling the lot behind the cafeteria. Arlen groaned. "Oh, man, they're getting ready for Organization Day. All the frat boys and their sorority girls will be here setting up booths." West Campus Drive was closed. Edna looked puzzled, so Arlen continued. "Every semester, campus clubs set up tables, build booths and stuff, and recruit. It's kind of a big deal."

"We can't make it to the library on foot. My mom's ankle won't make it."

From under the tarp, Edna said, "And I could use a bathroom."

"Me too," Arlen chimed in.

"Okay, they'll have the cafeteria unlocked to help the set-up. We'll park the truck and mingle for a while. That's actually good. We'll let the excitement of the bodies die down."

"I'm filthy. We all are," Walt's mother said.

Arlen picked a "staff only" spot on the edge of the parking lot, parked, and climbed out of the truck. No one seemed to notice that two of the four people crawled out from under a tarp. The sound of hammers and cheerful chatter filled the night.

Walt thought for a minute. "We've been assembling a booth for, uh, the Young Republicans."

"Works for me. But I'm surprised they haven't shut down the whole campus." Jane looked at the bustling students carrying lumber, painting signs, and throwing Frisbees. "Normal protocol calls for a large, secure perimeter. Maybe they think it's under control."

"Or maybe the people making that decision are more interested in us, because they know who killed Thibert and Darden." Walt sounded like he didn't want to believe it.

Jane closed her eyes. "You think of the nicest things."

"Okay, bathrooms are inside the cafeteria, on the left. We'll meet up out here."

They all went inside the building except for Walt, who lounged against a wall to keep an eye on the crowd. He was as tired as he'd ever been in his life. He didn't like that—from past experience, he knew that fatigue made him prone to haste and errors, and this was more important than any test, even the SAT. He scrubbed at his face, took a deep breath, and scanned the crowd again. Jane came back, and he took his turn. When he came out, she was waiting, and she didn't even look tired. It wasn't fair. Neither Arlen nor Edna were in sight.

"Uh-oh." Jane pointed to the parking lot, where a black Road Runner was turning in. "We need to run."

"We can't leave my mom."

"Walt, we can't get back to the truck. He's spotted it. And Minkoff is probably somewhere close." She studied the milling crowd for a moment. "Okay, I've got an idea." She hurried over to one of the girls making crepe paper flowers for the archway that would eventually frame the cafeteria doors and spoke to her urgently. In a moment, she came back and said, "Go."

Walt didn't move. "What did you tell her?"

"I said I was a Tri Delt from Cal State LA, here to get ideas for our Organization Fair, and that a man was following me. Our advisor was in the ladies' room. I described your mother and asked the girl if she would tell her when she came out that Walt and Jane said to wait."

"Quick thinking. But Morovich can get my mom. And she won't know to play along with what this sorority girl tells her."

"Don't underestimate your mother. She's really something."

"Yeah, but—"

"It's still a good idea. We just have to make sure he sees us running."

"That won't be hard. Here he comes." Walt pointed, and indeed, the fireplug figure of Morovich was heading for them, pushing through the crowd. Somewhere he'd picked up a navy-blue pea coat. The baggy wool coat hung lower on one side. Walt was afraid he knew why.

A moment later, they were sprinting across the grass, passing the Student Union excavation, heading for the library. The early morning crowds were beginning to fill the quad. That didn't keep Walt from spotting Minkoff standing on the balcony of the closest building and scanning the crowd—he was the only one in a leisure suit. They hooked left and headed for the construction. When Walt looked back over his shoulder, Minkoff was gone. Sawhorses blocked the way down into the excavation. Jane put one hand on the crosspiece and smoothly vaulted over the barricade with a quick flash of leg; Walt slipped under. They slid down the dirt slope to the bottom of the excavation and ran into the jungle of pipes and boards, with Morovich right behind them. They rolled under a water truck, crawled out the other side, crouched behind a giant tire, and were hidden for the moment, Walt panting and Jane not even breathing hard and grinning.

"We may have to break in to the library. I don't think we dare wait for them to open." Jane sounded worried.

"Here's a question," Walt said, panting.

"You always have questions, don't you?"

"Well, of course, yeah." He looked genuinely puzzled. She waved her hand in a "come on" gesture. "Oh, okay. Why is he chasing us? No, why are *they* chasing us. We have to assume Minkoff saw us from the balcony."

Jane was down on her knees, watching under the truck for the approach of feet. She pushed the edge of her flip away from her face and didn't look up at Walt. "What do you mean? They want the book. He has to get back that proof of death or go to prison. And those stories you hear about cops in jail? All true."

"I get it. But why not just follow us, let us get the book for him, and then take it away? That's what I would do under the circumstances."

She grinned. "Maybe he's not that smart?"

"I think there's something else."

Now she looked up, brushing her hair back again. "Yeah, well, if you figure it out, and I bet you will, make sure you let me know." Walt looked at her carefully. She shook her head. "And no, I don't know why. Unless—" Her grin faded.

Walt rubbed his eyes, frowning. She noticed and then went back to looking for Morovich or Thibert. He said, "He knows you saw him kill Becky. And he's certain you told me. And you're a cop, so you'll be believed. He has to kill you, book or no book."

"Somehow, in all the rush, I hadn't thought of that. But you know, I didn't actually see him pull the trigger. I mean, he was there, I ducked, and Becky went down on top of me. I just heard the blast. In court, I couldn't swear that he killed her."

"Well, great, all we have to do is tell him that, and he'll leave us alone. Look, all this goes away when we get the book and he goes to jail."

She licked her lips. "Okay, look, when he finds us, I'll keep him occupied. You get to the library and get that book."

"No!"

"Yes! Look, I know how it sounds, but he won't kill me right away, and he sure won't do it here with all those kids around. You get the book, get to the cops, and they can find me."

"Jane, we talked about this. What if I run into a crooked cop? I'm dead."

"You have to read the names in the book and find a cop who isn't in it."

There was something wrong with this, but Walt couldn't put his finger on it. He was tired, so tired. What was that? "Shhh!" He heard a noise that was not part of the usual chatter and laughter of a campus at the start of a fine fall day. Then a grinning Morovich stepped around the corner of the scaffolding. Morovich opened his coat to show them the sawed-off shotgun hanging from a leather holster and a small revolver stuffed into the waistband of his cords. He gave them a mocking bow and waved Walt up the hill, in the direction of the library. Jane shoved Walt to his feet and ran at Morovich. Walt ran, listening for a gunshot or the flat bark of a shotgun, but he heard neither.

He made it up the hill to the library, out of breath and dizzy, and rested for a moment, hands on his knees. There was the usual knot of students gathered around the main entrance, waiting for the doors to be unlocked. He was not entirely surprised to see Needra there.

She handed him a cup of coffee from the machines and sipped on her own. Machine coffee was always bad, but this was awful. He drank it anyway. "You look like crap," she said cheerily.

"Thanks." He finished the lukewarm coffee and started to feel a little better. Behind him, he heard the doors being unlocked.

The crowd poured inside, Walt along with them, and he hustled up the stairs to the third floor, to the PS section, with Needra trailing along.

Unlike the Dewey Decimal System, big academic libraries organize their collection by the Library of Congress system, which uses a combination of letters and numbers. PS is devoted to American Literature. Walt turned down the first row and saw Arlen was in the stacks, rummaging through the shelves of books, opening them, discarding them.

"Arlen!"

"Walt!"

Walt looked down at the book in Arlen's hands and then at the stack by his feet. "I'm glad you're here," his friend said and then blurted out, "I can't find it."

"Arlen, why did you ditch us?"

"What are you talking about? I said I'd go on ahead. You didn't hear me? I said it when we were in the cafeteria."

"No, somehow I missed that. No luck yet, huh?"

"I was smart enough to get this far."

Walt frowned, wondering what Arlen meant, but he was starting to fade, fatigue tugging at his entire body.

"Where's Jane and your mom?"

"We sort of got separated." *And Jane's probably safe until Morovich gets the book. I hope.* "You figured out what PS meant."

"I remembered Becky was a student assistant in the library, and last semester, I was an English lit major, and 'PS' had to be the start of a call number. But these are all real library books." He paused. "I wonder. Oh, man, I wonder if somebody else found it, saw that it wasn't a real library book, and turned it in, like to lost and found or something? It might be in the trash. Look, Walt, why don't you check that while I finish up here?"

He hasn't gotten the last part yet.

Walt shook his head. "If somebody turned it in, whoever on the library staff examined it would see Polaroids of dead people. They'd have turned it over to the campus cops, and Morovich would know."

"Man, I hope you're right."

"Almost certainly spiral-bound, about four inches by six. I'm not sure what color the cover is."

"Red. The cover's red."

"Arlen, how do you know that?"

His friend licked his lips. "I heard it somewhere. You know, I used to go up to the crashpad every once in a while. There were chicks, and they usually had some bitchin' weed."

"Why didn't you say this before? Never mind. So you knew Becky?"

"The dead girl? No, not very well, but people talked about her, things like she worked in the library and once she smoked a lot of Acapulco and had the munchies and ate a whole box of Wheaties. Shit like that, you know."

"Who else did you know up there?"

"A bunch of guys, just people to hang with. Walt, you gotta admit you're not much of a party guy."

"Who talked about Becky?"

"I don't know, everybody. Uh, wait, Walt, why the third degree? Hey, man, I'm on your side." Walt waited, and Arlen added, "Okay, okay, there was this one hippie chick, little round glasses, granny dresses."

"Beads? Long brown hair?"

"Yeah, sure, that's her. I think her name was Needra. Why?"

"Later. All right. It's in the PS category. Look for call numbers that have PS912. Be methodical; we can't do this twice."

"How did you . . .? Never mind."

A moment later, Arlen said, "Walt, how about this?" He held out a large volume.

"It's the right size, but—bingo!" Walt held up a battered textbook—*English Literature to 1500*. "This call number isn't right. It's hand-printed." He flipped the textbook open and, in a hollowed-out space where the center of the pages used to be, a small spiral-bound notebook rested. It was red with brown stains on the cover and the edges of the pages. It was thicker than it should have been. When Walt opened it to the first page, the way he always opened a book, he saw an almost illegible scrawl, but it seemed to be a name with a schedule of activities and a dollar amount at the bottom. He took a deep breath and turned the page.

There was a Polaroid snapshot glued to the second page. The man in the snapshot was obviously dead. His throat was cut, and an impossible amount of blood covered his chest. His face was clear. Morovich was bending over the body. Walt flipped to the last page with a snapshot glued to it. It showed a young man with a bullet hole between his eyes lying in a cement trench. Walt thought two things at once. One, that the dead kid was probably the one found in the trench leading up to the sculpture called *Hardfact* and, two, that the hole in his forehead was certainly a bullet hole. He'd seen one before, in Stanley Thibert's forehead. *Small caliber. Probably a .22.*

"You did it," Arlen said. "Look, Walt, there's some things I have to tell you."

"Like Needra, the hippie chick, told you Becky had the notebook and that it was important."

"How did you know?"

"Needra was looking for the book the day she and I got into the crashpad. And you knew all this and didn't tell me."

"I wanted to be the one to find the book. You know, save the day."

"I don't understand."

Arlen looked at Walt, and something in his face changed, became harder. He stood straighter. "Of course not. You wouldn't. You're special, got Berkeley in your future. Everybody knows you're some kind of genius. Marty's a football star, has been since high school. Me? You know how I get dates? Girls want to be close to Marty, so they go with me on double dates. Yeah, that's my high school love life. Then there was Needra."

Walt had no idea what to say. Arlen seemed to be saying that he envied Walt, but that was impossible. "Arlen, listen, you're a good guy."

"You know what it's like being around two guys who are special and you're not?"

"At least you had dates!"

Walt's world spun. He saw his past in short clips—getting pushed down, books ruined. Hey, look, new white tennies! Let's stomp on 'em, break 'em in right. Date? Yeah, right. Extracurricular activities? Secretary of the audiovisual club because nobody else would do it and there were only six members anyway. It had never once entered his mind that anyone could envy him. It still didn't seem real.

And then the hippie chick herself stepped around the corner and into their row of stacks.

Red-faced, Arlen went over to Needra and slipped his arm around her waist. Walt saw the look on his friend's face and knew with absolute certainty what was going to happen next. He didn't know how he knew, but he was sure. He wanted desperately to prevent it, but before he could speak, Arlen said proudly, "We're going steady. How about that, huh? We're in love, so I had to help her. Sorry, Walt, but that's the way it is. I want the notebook. I promised Needra."

Needra looked up at him. "Arlen, sweetie, don't get carried away. I needed your help, so I traded a little making out for it. No big deal, okay? Now I want the notebook." She shrugged Arlen's arm off.

Walt thought he would remember Arlen's face for the rest of his life.

A life that might be very short unless he got the notebook to the cops, and Jane, something about Jane, and the coffee wasn't helping . . . He was tired, so tired.

"Why do you want it?" Walt asked.

"Why? Because it shows pigs murdering people just like we always said, all right? I'm giving, well, selling it to the *LA Times*. Some bread for me and socking it to the Establishment."

"Morovich says he'll hurt my family."

"He'll get arrested or something first, and it'll all work out. I'm sure it will, and I'll get some bread, and we'll really stick it to the Man."

"Needra, it needs to go to the cops. I have to give it to Jane. I'll give you credit for finding it, okay?"

"No, I'm taking it."

"Needra, I'm not giving it to you." Walt blinked. He was very tired, more fatigued than he had ever been in his life. It was time to end this. End this. Right. He stuffed the notebook down the back of his jeans, pushed by her, and took the stairs down to the first floor. He had to hold on to the railing to keep his balance, and he was having a difficult time focusing his thoughts.

Arlen was next to him. "Walt, I need to tell you something." But Arlen was speaking from a long way away. Walt made it out the double doors and to the lawn before he stumbled and went to his knees. *My mother will have a hard time getting the grass stains out. No, these clothes are ruined anyway.* It had been a very long day. But at least he had the notebook everybody was looking for.

He sprawled on the lawn. All he could see was a pair of dirty feet in scuffed leather sandals—he knew the brand name of the sandals; it began with a B, but he couldn't think of it—and when, with a huge effort, he turned his head the other way, he saw the cuffs of Arlen's white jeans and his black Chuck Taylors, then his knees, and then his face, looking surprised, as Arlen toppled to the grass next to him.

"Wake up. Walter Dalrymple, wake up." Just as he was getting to sleep. Maybe if he ignored them, they'd go away. These all-nighters in the lab were killing him. Whoever it was didn't go away. Instead, a hand began shaking his shoulder. He forced his eyes open and found that he was lying on the grass in front of the library, staring at a pair of polished black boots. *Aha! More shoes.* That seemed important.

And the person shaking him, who had now stepped back, was a khaki-uniformed campus cop.

Walt sat up. His mouth was dry, his eyes grainy, and he had grass stuck to his left cheek.

"Walter Dalrymple?"

"Um, yeah, sure, why not?"

For some reason, the campus cop looked confused. But that was all right. Walt was used to confusing people. So he blundered on. "No matter. Right. I've got it. Glad to see you. I'm Walt." He thought for a minute. "Yes, I'm Walter. Call me Walt. And you are?"

"Walter Darlymple, you're under arrest for trespassing, assaulting a police officer, and, after Long Beach cops get to you, accessory to murder. Get up." The cop, not much taller than Walt, face pocked from serious bouts with acne, and with a toothpick projecting from the corner of his mouth, bent over Walt and tugged at his arm.

That cleared Walt's head. "What? Wait, I don't understand, but I have the notebook everybody's looking for. Who are you?" He saw the cop's face change and realized that nobody had ever said the only cops involved were Long Beach. No reason a campus cop couldn't be part of the ring, no reason at all.

"My name is Livingston. Give me the notebook."

"Dr. Livingston, I presume?" Walt laughed and brushed the grass off his cheek. The cop didn't laugh.

Of course the red notebook with the pictures of dead people and at least one person who wanted him dead, that notebook, was no longer stuffed down the back of his pants.

"Where's Arlen? He has on white jeans."

"No idea who you're talking about. The notebook."

"Um, I lost it."

"Sure, kid, sure. You lost it. Get up. Hey, it'll be okay. I wasn't serious about those charges."

"And I was working with an undercover police officer, and you better not do anything bad, because they'll be looking for me, they really will."

The cop was smiling now, but his grip on Walt's arm was painful. "We just want to ask you some questions. Up. Get up. We're going to my car and then down to Campus Police for questioning, that's all. You behave, and you'll be fine." He was speaking loudly for the audience of students gathered to watch the excitement.

Walt looked around, but there was no sign of anyone he knew. No Arlen, no mother—he was glad of that—and no Jane. And of course, no Needra. He licked his dry lips and was getting ready to yell for help when the cop hauled him to his feet and whispered, "Kid, we both know you're thinking about yelling a shitload of stupid stuff, am I right? Do it, and some of these kids will get hurt bad. I got nothing to lose, can you dig it? Not a thing. So come along quietly." Walt went.

"Water, please." There was a drinking fountain next to the food machines outside of LH-151, where he had watched the suits look for him only a couple of days ago, in another lifetime. The cop dragging him along shrugged and hauled him in that direction. A freak with thin brown hair parted in the middle and hanging down to his shoulders, wearing bellbottom jeans, a leather vest, no shirt, and a chicken-bone necklace, stepped up and stood in front of them. "Hey, man, where you taking him? What's he done?"

"None of your business. Get out of the way, long-hair, before this turns ugly."

"Yeah?" The freak hooked both thumbs behind his wide leather belt. "Look around, pig." And all at once, there were at least a dozen kids, all in jeans and sandals, standing silently, just looking at Walt and the cop. Walt felt the cop hesitate and then make up his mind. His free hand dropped to the gun holstered at his side.

Walt started chattering. "No, wait, it's okay, really. My name's Walter Dalrymple, and I'm just answering some questions." He spelled his name. "His name is Livingston. I'm a physics major, and there was a problem in one of the labs. It's fine now, yeah, fine now, but thanks for helping."

Walt got to the fountain and tried to think as he slurped up water. He splashed water on his face and the back of his neck. Time! He needed time to think. He didn't get it. After three slurps and one more face splash, the cop pulled him up. As he dragged Walt up the walkway, toward the parking lot, Livingston whispered, "Smart move, kid." Walt wasn't so sure. He couldn't decide where he would be shot while trying to escape, but he was sure that was the plan unless he could think of something. Unfortunately, his brain was still sluggish, not really functioning the way he was used to.

"Too many people have seen me with you, and back there, they know my name, and now they know yours. If you do anything to me, you'll get caught."

"Maybe, maybe. But who'll listen to a bunch of freaks? Am I right about that? You bet I am. Their kind is destroying society." Livingston spat out the toothpick, immediately replaced it with a fresh one from his shirt pocket. "Long hairs like that. And nobody cares, so I figure, why not get it while the getting's good? Only, how was I to know somebody was keeping records?" He shook his head. "Did you look in the notebook?"

"No!"

"Liar, liar, pants on fire. Kid, you looked." They were in the staff parking lot now, between the library and West Campus Drive, heading toward a campus police car sitting in the middle of an aisle. Walt began to struggle, pulling futilely at his arm.

"That's right, kid, try to get away. That's how I gotta do you. See, you pull a gun, point it at me, so I shoot. Nothing personal."

Well, at least I've got a minute to think.

Livingston tongued the toothpick over to the other side of his mouth and muttered, "Here's as good as anywhere else," before he pushed Walt against the side of a dusty Ford Econoline van, held him with his forearm as he bent, lifted up his khaki cuff, and pulled a small revolver out of his boot.

I wasn't supposed to hear the last. So much for a minute to think.

Livingston flipped the little revolver open and deftly shook the shells out into his shirt pocket. "Here, take it, kid." At first, Walt wouldn't touch the gun. Then he gripped it and, without warning, swung with all his might and caught the cop in the side of the face. It was so unexpected that even though Walt didn't pack much of a punch at the best of times and now he was groggy, half asleep, the punch was enough that the campus cop staggered back, tripped, and sat down hard with blood pouring from his mouth.

Toothpick stuck him. Good.

But he kept a tight grip on Walt's jacket as he did and pulled him down too. They both landed on the blacktop, the cop reaching for his gun, Walt struggling to get free, until, finally a memory of playground scuffles surfaced, and he grabbed one of the cop's fingers and bent it back till he heard a snap. Livingston screamed and let go of Walt's jacket. Walt got to his feet and ran for his life, heading for West Campus Drive.

Actually, given his lack of sleep and physical condition after the events of the night, it was more of a stumble than a run, with the cop after him, clutching his injured hand to his chest and screaming, "Halt or I'll shoot!"

Perfect. This is just what he wanted.

A faded red VW Beetle rattled up the street with the passenger door open. Needra leaned over and yelled, "Walt! Here, quick!" He ran to the Beetle and dove in. She had it in gear and was rolling before he got his left foot off the pavement, but he made it, twisted around, and slammed the door. He looked back to see Livingston running, but not after them. He was sprinting toward the other side of the parking lot. Needra said, "I looked inside the book. I wish I hadn't. Those were pictures of dead people! I wish I hadn't looked. It was awful! I wish I had a joint."

What had she expected? Walt was adjusting the rear-view mirror so he could keep an eye out for pursuit. "That seems to be the consensus. The awful part, not the joint. Where's the notebook?"

She shook her head. "I hid it, man. I hid it again. I had to. Who knows who we can trust?"

"This has gone far enough. I don't know where my mother is, my father is freaking out with a gun, and now it looks like at least one campus cop is involved. We have to take a chance. If we tell a whole bunch of campus cops, they can't *all* be in on it."

"How do you feel?"

"Fuzzy."

"I put six reds in your coffee. Crunched them up first and mixed them in, and you never noticed."

"I was tired. And you did Arlen too, didn't you?"

"The look on his face when he realized, it was outta sight, or, you know, kind of sad too, but you know, I had to do it, for the people."

You know how I get dates? Girls want to be close to Marty, so they go with me on double dates. He wondered if Arlen was okay.

The street was open and Organization Day was in full swing. She downshifted for the turn at the bottom of the hill. "Are you sure? About the cops, I mean?" They were down the hill now, approaching the turn that would take them into the parking lot where he had seen Morovich and then Minkoff and Thibert, before he'd gotten the ride with the hippies. He wondered if they'd liked the free concert. The parking lot outside of Campus Police was where he would tell his story and see what happened. He wished he had the notebook. He wished he had a better idea.

Needra repeated, "Are you sure about the cops?"

"No, of course not. But I can't think of anything else. If we take it to the papers, they'll try to verify it, and that will take time, and my guess is a lot of witnesses will disappear. It has to get to the cops somehow."

Needra hauled the wheel, and the Beetle swerved around the corner and into the lot, the air-cooled motor echoing off rows of parked cars. "I marched, you know, end the war and all that, and I knew the Establishment was bad, but I guess I didn't really understand just how bad it is. I didn't understand." The Beetle slowed as she started crying. "When I was l-little, my mom always said, you know, 'If you're lost or anything, just find a p-policeman.' She always said that." All at once, she was crying harder, trying to drive with one hand and swipe at her eyes with the other, smearing black mascara all the way back to her ear. "They took it all away, and I'll never feel like that again, safe, you know? Never again. I marched, you know? I really believed it, but I guess I didn't get it, you know." Her voice trailed off. "It doesn't make sense."

"That cop that was hauling me away said hippies are, quote, 'destroying society,' end quote."

"I wish I had a joint."

"My mom said the same thing—"

"She wanted a joint?" Needra grinned feebly.

"—about police, and look, it's almost always true. These guys are the exception, not the rule. They're criminals."

"If you're wrong, we're dead."

"Needra, just let me off in the parking lot. I'll take it from there."

"You don't even know where the book is. Besides, they know I've got it. If we don't stop them, I'll be on their list too."

Walt was sure that given time, he could come up with a counterargument, but Needra was sliding the bug to a stop in front of the police station, missing the downshift and stalling when she popped the clutch. He was not entirely surprised to see his mother, Arlen, and Jane come running out. He and Needra got out and there was a minute when everybody was talking at the same time.

"We were so worried."

"We couldn't find you."

"Walt, I'm sorry, man. I'm sorry. I just wanted . . ." Arlen looked at Needra, and his voice trailed off.

"I need to tell you about your father."

"I got away from Morovich when some of the fraternity guys showed up."

Then Walt said, "We have to end this right now. Needra knows where the book is. We're going inside and telling the whole story to a group, to as many cops as we can. They can't all be in on it."

"You hope," Jane said.

He turned on her. "That's right. I *hope*. What I *know* is we're out of other options. Morovich is hunting us now. He doesn't seem to care about the book anymore."

Jane sighed. "You're right. I can't even call it in, because I'm not sure who to tell. Too many people know now. Unless he kills us all and gets away with it, he's fucked." Edna pursed her lips at the language, but Jane didn't notice. "My job was only to implicate or clear Morovich. But it's gotten bigger than that."

Walt was only half-listening. "You know, I wonder about Minkoff. Where does he fit? He's pretty clearly involved. And why did Morovich kill Thibert?"

"The old guy in the leisure suit? He saw me outside the crashpad and asked me a bunch of questions, him and his partner. They're in the pictures, both of them." Needra was recovering; she almost sounded normal. "Yeah, Walt's right. Let's do this."

Then her eyes widened, and she said, "Oh." There was a sharp Crack! Like two boards being slapped together, and a spot of red bloomed on the front of her dress, bright red spreading over the lavender paisley. Her knees buckled, and Needra, sometimes known as Rabbit, slumped into Walt's arms. As he was lowering her to the ground, Jane reacted, pushing Mrs. Dalrymple down and pulling a small revolver out of her purse. There was another crack and dark moisture blossomed on the waist of Jane's dress, and she went down to one knee. She clutched her side with one hand, tugged on his pants with the other, and said, "Walt, get down, get down."

"Needra's hurt."

"I know. I know. Get down."

Seconds after the shots, cops boiled out of the station, looking everywhere. Had there really been gunshots on a college campus? Those cops who had guns kept them holstered.

Jane's wasn't. She scanned the parking lot as another shot chipped asphalt at her feet. This convinced the campus cops that they needed to do something. Two ran toward Walt and company, approaching cautiously after they saw Jane's gun. "Police officer!

Long Beach PD," she yelled, clutching at her side, crawling over to Walt to shelter him behind her body.

Then Leonard Minkoff played out his endgame. He stood up from his hiding place behind a green Ford pickup and pointed a gun at everybody. "Police officer! I'm a police officer! He held up a badge. Everybody down on the ground!" Then he shot at Walt, but Jane was there, pushing Walt aside again and taking a second bullet, this one grazing her calf. Minkoff saw one of the cops draw his weapon, aimed his gun at him and pulled the trigger. He missed. It was the last thing he did. Before he could get a shot off, he was riddled with bullets. He twisted as he was hit again and again, before falling down behind the truck.

As Walt held Needra, a Long Beach police car backed out of its parking spot and stopped between Walt, Jane, and the police. Walt's mother slid across the bench seat and opened the passenger door. He gently laid Needra's head down, grabbed his mother's arm and pulled her out so they were on the pavement behind the car while, around them, the pleasant morning was filled with shouts as the cops looked for other shooters. "Mom, it's over. It's okay."

"No, no, it isn't. That's what I need to tell you. It's not, it's not over. Your father is on his way from Oceanside. I mean, he's probably here by now. He has a gun, Walter. He has a gun, and I don't know what he's going to do."

"Mom—"

"I think he wants to kill that man."

"Morovich. Got to be the crazy guy. How does he know about him?"

"I don't know. He's not in his right mind, really. He got more pictures of your sister at school and a really ugly note about you and how you had to find the book, and your father went crazy. He says the only way to keep her safe is for Morovich to be dead. He's crazy, son." Walt wasn't sure who she meant—Morovich or his father—and decided it really didn't matter. "And he's got a gun." *That doesn't narrow it down, since they both have guns.* He felt an insane urge to share this insight with his mother, but he fought it down. "I don't want him to shoot anybody," his mother continued, "and I don't want Penny hurt either."

Jane whispered, "Help me into the car. First aid kit." Walt didn't ask why they weren't going to the police station. The car, a two-year-old Ford, was sitting there with its passenger door open and the engine running.

Needra's dead. Jane's hurt. The car's running. Okay, here we go. One more time.

"Mom, we need a distraction." All of this took place while more of the police cautiously emerged from the police station with weapons drawn.

Edna nodded. She braced herself with one hand on the tire, got to her feet, and limped toward the police with her arms raised. "Oh, help, I don't feel well." She staggered, clutched at her chest, and then the middle-aged lady in the dirty black pantsuit collapsed dramatically to the blacktop. They rushed to her and started taking her pulse, asking her questions.

Walt got Jane to her feet and half-dragged her into the car. She took the keys out of the ignition and got the first aid kit out of the trunk. Then she carefully lowered herself into the passenger seat, grimacing, and tossed him the keys. "Drive. If the cops get to your dad first, they won't understand, and it could be really bad."

"You're hurt!"

"No shit, Sherlock." She tore open a gauze packet with her teeth. "Sorry. It's not bad. Look, I'll be okay. But there's no way we could explain and make them understand, not fast enough."

"Yeah, but, Jane, we need police to end this."

"Turn on the bubs."

"What?" She reached over and turned the lights and siren on. All of the cops gathered around his mother looked up, startled. Some started walking briskly toward the car, hands on holsters. "Don't worry, they'll be there."

"Oh, man." But he ran around to the driver's side and slammed the cruiser into gear, and they flew out of the parking lot.

Jane ripped the hole in the side of her dress, enlarging it so she could see the wound. Then she groped in the kit and swabbed brown stuff on it as they turned onto State College Drive. She applied a small dressing and moved on to the wound on her calf. She turned off the siren. "We have more problems," she said as she pressed a bandage to her calf.

"Oh, you mean more than my dad going crazy and looking for a guy who's *really* crazy and they both have guns? More than that? More? You want more?" He laughed a little hysterically. "Oliver Twist. I think I was the only one in my class who read anything other than the Classics Illustrated comic book."

"Walt, stay cool, all right? I need you to stay cool here."

"Sure, no problem at all, except that my dad's gone apeshit and wants to shoot a guy who's even crazier and, and . . ."

Jane looked at him oddly, but she grasped the steering wheel and gently moved the car to the right. "Pick one lane and stick with it, okay?"

"Yeah, okay, cool. I'm cool." He took a deep breath as he slid through the light and made the left turn onto Bellflower. "What problems?"

"We've done a lot of stuff that's, um, illegal. And the people who understand are dead."

"Hey, my mom and Arlen."

"Are good, but it's hearsay. We need the book."

"Great. Well, look on the bright side. If Morovich shoots us, we won't have to worry about it." Traffic parted ahead of them, and they were in front of the Beachi Tiki in minutes.

He pulled the police car into the parking lot and jumped out. Jane got out more slowly, favoring her side. By the time they were through the breezeway and heading up the stairs she was holding on to his arm.

"Are you sure you're all right?"

She ignored his question. "Okay, where did Needra say she left the book?" He looked at her. "My God, you don't trust me."

"I'm sorry, Jane, it's just all confusing. I'm sorry. She didn't say, not precisely. Okay, she didn't say at all, but it's gotta be the crashpad."

"Don't be sorry. You're learning. Okay, why the crashpad?"

"It's close, and she could get in, and something tells me Morovich is there too."

"Yeah, I think so too. Okay, time to choose. Do you trust me? And you need to pick before we get to the top of the stairs. And Walt," She paused, and her eyes got wide. "Oh, boy." She slumped down, leaning against the wall. She looked up at him and grinned. There was blood on her teeth. "Doesn't matter now. Oh, man, sorry, Walt, I thought I could do this, but I'm, uh, I'm in deeper trouble here than I thought."

He knelt next to her. "Jane, give me the gun."

Her eyelids fluttered. She grinned again. "Who you gonna shoot? Me or him?" But she held the gun out butt first. "Either way, it's been a great run."

There were sirens in the distance. "You're gonna be fine, Jane. Hang on. And it was always you I trusted. Always." He slipped the gun back into her limp hand. "Hold on to this. Just in case. Make sure he doesn't get down the stairs."

"Count on it."

He crept up to the third floor. The door to the crashpad was standing open. He could hear indistinct voices. He slipped along the walkway and peered in through the crack next to the hinges. He saw his father, Tom, pointing a gun at Morovich. The latter was holding the red notebook in one hand and a badge in the other.

Bad cops have badges; the good one doesn't. Perfect.

His father said, "You're the bastard who threatened my daughter."

"Sir, put the gun down slowly." Morovich took a step toward Walt's father.

It was an easy mistake to make. Morovich was doing his cop thing, so calm and soothing that Walt's first thought was: *It's going to be all right.* His father had the gun. He stepped out into the doorway and said, "Dad, it's okay," except his father turned at the sound, and Morovich moved quickly. He grabbed Tom's wrist and twisted it viciously until Walt heard a distinct snap. Then Morovich forced the older man to his knees, and he had the gun, and he was pointing it at Walt, and all at once, Walt was going to lose. After everything, after all of the running and hiding and Needra getting shot, it wasn't going to work, not like in a James Bond or a Shell Scott story. *He'll shoot Jane too, on the way out. Unless she's dead already.*

"Come in, kid. Right now."

Walt did as he was told, walking in, standing in front of the stereo, and trying not to look at the expression on his father's face. The sirens were louder. "Yeah, I hear 'em too. We need to finish this pronto. But we have a little time—protocol dictates that they won't rush the building until they have an idea of what they're up against. They'll get on a bullhorn and tell everybody to get out of the crashpad or face arrest. Remember, they don't know about me yet." He took a revolver out of his coat pocket and then slipped Tom's automatic behind his belt.

He's got a small gun, probably the one he used to kill Thibert. Why not the shotgun? Oh, right, he has to kill us with a police weapon. He couldn't explain a shotgun.

"Yes, they do. I told them everything."

"Who will they believe? A heroic undercover cop, risking his life every day to keep society from falling apart or some college kid? This is tragic, of course, and there will be an investigation, and I may take early retirement, but I can make it work. I know—"

Walt finished the thought for him. "Where the bodies are buried. Literally."

"Yep."

"It won't work."

"Your dad ran in waving a gun. He was nuts, and unfortunately, when you showed up, he shot you by mistake. I was trying to talk him down, but after that, I had to put one in him."

There would be a lot of questions, but it might work, especially if Jane died alone in the stairwell. Walt didn't like to think about that. On the stairs. Alone. His eyes flicked to the corner where the cheap stereo sat on top of the cinderblock and board bookcase. Tick, tick. Come on in.

Walt had one thought, one card, so he played it.

He turned. "You'll have to shoot me in the back." All at once, Walt's legs decided they'd had it. He fell against the stereo, stumbling, and in the process, he clutched a record, dragging it from the top of the untidy stack.

And in that moment, as Walt got ready to play his last, desperate card, he realized he'd been wrong about the few really dangerous ones—they didn't stuff you head first into a hamper full of wet gym towels because they were jealous of emotions you felt that were unknown to them. Oh, maybe at first, but that really didn't get it, oh no. Points off for incomplete answer.

They liked it.

"Turn around, kid."

As Morovich stepped forward to shoot him, Walt turned and whipped the LP like a Frisbee as hard as he could, right at the cop's face. Morovich fired the gun, but it's almost impossible not to flinch when something's flying at your face. He missed. The sharp edge of the record caught him squarely on the bridge of the nose, splitting skin, spraying blood into the air in a wide fan as Morovich brought the gun up again. Then Tom Dalrymple, ignoring his broken wrist, lashed out with a foot at the side of Morovich's knee. Morovich stumbled but stayed on his feet until Walt's father drove his wingtip into the injured knee again, and Walt heard another snap, louder than the one he'd heard when his father's wrist was broken. The leg crumpled under Morovich, and he went down on his back, and Walt was on him, the memory of playground fights guiding him to land on his enemy's arms with all his weight on his knees. And that's one thing about mice: they don't fight often, but when they do, it's all out, a desperate attack driven by reckless abandon and total disregard for safety or anything else. As Morovich tried to raise the gun, Walt rocked back, grinding biceps under his knees, grabbing not the wrist that held the gun but rather the gun's cylinder—one of his heroes, Shell Scott or James Bond, had done that, saying that the cylinder had to turn before the gun could fire. There was a moment when they struggled, and Walt saw the hammer going back on the weapon and felt his adrenaline-fueled strength fading. Morovich was slowly pulling the gun free. Walt rocked again and heard Morovich groan as the pain spread from his biceps, but he kept pulling the gun free.

Then a drop of blood landed on Morovich's face. He blinked as another fell into his eyes. Walt yanked the gun free as a bloody hand and forearm appeared and pressed a gun against the cop's temple. Jane sank down next to them, grinning and trying to say something as the room filled with men with guns. Protocol apparently goes out the window when someone steals a police car and drives away at high speed with the siren wailing.

They needed to call a second ambulance because there were three people to be transported. Walt insisted on riding with Jane. And his father.

And anyway, Morovich could wait.

From her bed at Long Beach Memorial, Jane said, "Sorry about the dance. I can't believe you turned your back on Morovich."

Walt shrugged modestly. He was actually pretty proud of himself. "Playground experience. You have to develop a rear-view mirror. You learn to watch shadows so if somebody jumps you from behind, you can get out of the way. It's the same for reflective surfaces. I could see him, sort of, in the record. I had the LP in my hand, and I just turned and flipped it as hard as I could. I played Frisbee a lot. I mean, it's the only sport I've ever been good at. It's all—"

"In the wrist," she finished and laughed and then grimaced.

"If you pull those stitches loose, the doctor will be upset."

"Yeah."

"And on Friday, there's a new double feature at Los Altos."

"Why, Walter Dalrymple, are you asking me out on a date? And to a drive-in movie? A Passion Pit?"

"Well, I mean, I . . ." He straightened. "Yes. You bet I am. A date." He indicated her various dressings and his own. "Even if we have to watch the movie."

They didn't, at least not much.

And in the End . . .

The love you make, and take, is wonderful. There's never anything to replace that first feeling of *Oh my God, I'm in love.*

And February turned into March, and then, seemingly with no warning, finals were on him and his research was due for review.

In June, there was a knock, and when he opened the door of his apartment—Arlen and Marty were off on dates, separate dates—she was there with two pizza boxes.

She grinned. "Pizza Girl. She delivers."

"Jane, I have something to tell you."

"I know. Me, too."

He led her into the kitchen and got out paper plates before he took a deep breath and said, "I sent an abstract of my work to Berkeley, and they not only want me, they want me to attend a summer session. They've offered me a part-time job in the lab."

Jane nodded but didn't open the pizza boxes. "My transfer came through. LAPD, Hollenbeck division. I have to start in traffic, but that's okay."

"Jane, I-I . . ."

"Pizza girl, she delivers. But I have to run." She kissed him. "Walt, there's big things in store for you. I can tell. When you make your acceptance speech for the Nobel Prize, I want to be one of the people you thank." Before he could answer, she was out the door, leaving only a faint trace of perfume and pepperoni.

Leaving quickly had saved her. On the stairs, she brushed at her cheeks and sniffed once before hurrying down and climbing into Prince.

Walt was really not very hungry, but he looked at the pepperoni and black olive anyway. Maybe Arlen or Marty would eat some. When he lifted the second, smaller box, it felt light, like maybe it was empty, but he heard something slide around inside.

When he opened it, he saw a plastic magazine protector encasing a pristine copy of *Green Lantern #29*, the one Morovich had destroyed. There was something else in a small envelope, but he could hardly bear to look. At last, he slid his thumb under the flap and pulled it out. It was a Polaroid of her standing next to him. He had his arm around her waist and looked smug. He turned it over.

On the back, it said,

"Have a great summer vacation. Don't let your meat loaf.

Love,

Pizza Girl"

And beneath it was a perfect impression of hot pink lips.

When Arlen and Marty arrived, there were two slices of pizza left.

The End

See how Jane got started in law enforcement in *Buzzkill*.

About the author

James R. Preston spends most of his time at the keyboard, writing the award-winning Surf City Mysteries—think "beach noir." *Sailor Home From Sea* is the fifth novel in this series and was preceded by *Leave A Good-Looking Corpse, Read 'Em And Weep, The Road To Hell,* and *Pennies For Her Eyes.*

The Surf City Mysteries have been selected for inclusion in the California Detective Fiction collection of the Bancroft Library, one of the libraries at the University of California, Berkeley. You can read the opening chapter of each book at JamesRPreston.com.

Away from the keyboard, James likes reading, films (especially 1950's SF like *Them* and *The Crawling Eye*), sailing, bodyboarding, and Texas Hold'Em Poker. James played in one of the 2011 World Series tournaments and sadly busted out early. This year will be different.

Read 'Em And Weep

From the journals of T. R. Macdonald:

I was sort of hiding from two guys who either thought we were in business together or who wanted to kill me.

"Sort of hiding" because I could have left town and been relatively safe, but Las Vegas, NV, has so many wonderful things to see and do that I decided to go to a topless rollerskating show instead.

"Sort of hiding" because I was fairly sure that the guys in question would take Door Number Two and try to shoot me, a lot.

Why me? I'm T. R. Macdonald, a sort-of unemployed broker-analyst from the boutique—we handle a small number of very rich clients—firm of Fields, Smith, and Barkman. My sort-of girlfriend, Kandi, had asked me to go to Vegas to see if we could talk to her cousin Chet, because she thinks his adoptive father, Dr. Woodrow Shaw, may be nuts. Are you getting all this? There will be a quiz. Dr. Shaw asked me to go, too, and he offered to pay.

It sounded like easy money.

So I went.

I must be nuts.

The Road To Hell

From the journals of T. R. Macdonald:

I was standing in the desert, in the sun, outside of a semi-abandoned church, and I had a gun. My girlfriend, the lovely blonde Kandi Shaw, and I were registered in the Maiden's Blush Suite, one of the finest in Las Vegas' lavish Bromeliad Resort and Spa. Unfortunately, I wasn't in the suite. I was standing in the sun, waiting for my brains to finish boiling.

I'm T. R. Macdonald, a semi-unemployed broker-anaylst from Huntington Beach, California—Surf City, USA. And I was here instead of sitting on my short tri-fin outside the break line at the Huntington Pier because the casino offered me money to assist in security for WillieFest One, the richest slot tournament in history.

But so far I'd been mainly a moving target or punching bag—I was run off the road, chased by pit bulls, mixed it up with a vicious pimp, and was nearly trampled in a club stampede. Not to mention the part where I was poked in the nose. With a sawed-off shotgun. All of that led to the church, and my gun, and Kandi standing next to me with her gun in her hand—and she wanted to shoot somebody.

And if the two men inside the church didn't listen to reason, I was very much afraid she was right—I'd have to shoot them.

Pennies For Her Eyes

From the journals of T. R. Macdonald:

I was sitting on a wet bike in frigid water, watching waves the size of three-story buildings slide toward me, hump up, then hump up again getting even taller before crashing down with a sound like a Las Vegas casino imploding. I could be in one of those casinos, a fancy one, too, because they liked me and wanted me to work for them, or I could be on Wall Street moving around billion-dollar chunks of money.

But instead I was here, cold and anxious and very soon I'd have to drive the wet bike in front of one of these waves, dragging a beautiful redhead behind me on the end of a towline, and if -- when--she fell I'd have to go get her. Or die trying. That was the part I didn't like, the "die trying."

My name is T. R. Macdonald and believe it or not this was the good part. People hadn't started stuffing me in the trunks of cars or shooting at me. Yet.

Sailor Home From Sea

From the journals of T. R. Macdonald:

Westwood, CA.   A UCLA Teaching Assistant is killed in a hit-and-run accident. But it's not an accident. It's murder.

Chicago, IL.   A therapist at a prominent mental health clinic kills his girlfriend and then turns the gun on himself.

O'Hare International Airport Mary Shaw, aka Kandi, and the love of my life, is fleeing the scene of the murder-suicide when she is hacked. Her electronic life is destroyed and she is trapped with no ticket, no boarding pass, no cell phone, and no credit cards.

Huntington Beach, Surf City USA An artist named Mike Macdonald receives death threats. Mike's my father. Mike and Kandi need my help. The problem is, they don't want it. In fact, they don't want anything to do with me.

I'm down, but the surf's up.

www.ingramcontent.com/pod-product-compliance
Lightning Source LLC
Chambersburg PA
CBHW071009120726
47910CB00004B/1446